U0033915

FÜN學

美國英語閱讀課本 5

各學科實用課文 二版

+ **Workbook**

MP3
寂天雲 APP

AMERICAN
SCHOOL
TEXTBOOK

READING KEY

作者 Michael A. Putlack & e-Creative Contents　　譯者 丁宥暄

如何下載 MP3 音檔

❶ 寂天雲 APP 聆聽：掃描書上 QR Code 下載
「寂天雲 – 英日語學習隨身聽」APP。加入會員
後，用 APP 內建掃描器再次掃描書上 QR
Code，即可使用 APP 聆聽音檔。

❷ 官網下載音檔：請上「寂天閱讀網」
（www.icosmos.com.tw），註冊會員／登入後，
搜尋本書，進入本書頁面，點選「MP3 下載」
下載音檔，存於電腦等其他播放器聆聽使用。

The Best Preparation for Building
Academic Reading Skills and Vocabulary

The Reading Key series is designed to help students to understand American school textbooks and to develop background knowledge in a wide variety of academic topics. This series also provides learners with the opportunity to enhance their reading comprehension skills and vocabulary, which will assist them when they take various English exams.

Reading Key <Volume 1-3> is
a three-book series designed for beginner to intermediate learners.

Reading Key <Volume 4-6> is
a three-book series designed for intermediate to high-intermediate learners.

Reading Key <Volume 7-9> is
a three-book series designed for high-intermediate learners.

Features

- A wide variety of topics that cover American school subjects
  helps learners expand their knowledge of academic topics through interdisciplinary studies

- Intensive practice for reading skill development
  helps learners prepare for various English exams

- Building vocabulary by school subjects and themed texts
  helps learners expand their vocabulary and reading skills in each subject

- Graphic organizers for each passage
  show the structure of the passage and help to build summary skills

- Captivating pictures and illustrations related to the topics
  help learners gain a broader understanding of the topics and key concepts

Table of Contents

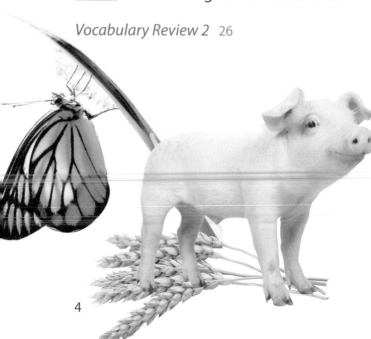

Chapter **3**
**Mathematics • Language •
Visual Arts • Music**

Workbook for Daily Review

Syllabus Vol. 5

Subject	Topic & Area	Title
Social Studies ★ **History and Geography**	World Geography	What Is a Globe?
	World Geography	Understanding Hemispheres
	Geography	The Environment of the West
	History	The California Gold Rush
	Geography	The Environment of the Southwest
	Economics	The Economy of the Southwest
	Geography	The Environment of the Southeast
	History	The Civil Rights Movement
	Geography	The Environment of the Northeast
	Economics	The Leading Industries of the Northeast
	Geography	The Midwest Region
	Geography	The Mountain States
Science	A World of Animals	How Do Animals Grow?
	A World of Animals	What Is Metamorphosis?
	Adaptations	How Do Animals Respond to Changes?
	Adaptations	Animal Adaptations for Survival
	Our Earth	What Changes Earth's Surface?
	Our Earth	Fast Changes to Earth's Surface
	The Universe	Our Solar System
	The Universe	The Sun and Other Stars
	Matter	What Is Matter?
	Matter	Changes in Matter
	Our Bodies	Taking Care of Our Bodies
	Our Bodies	The Six Nutrients
Mathematics	Fractions	Fractions
	Fractions	Understanding Fractions
	Decimals	Understanding Decimals
	Decimals	Reading and Writing Fractions and Decimals
Language and Literature	Myths	Norse Mythology
	Myths	Loki the Trickster
	Language Arts	What Kind of Sentence Is It?
	Language Arts	Punctuation Marks
Visual Arts	Visual Arts	Appreciating Artwork
	Visual Arts	Creating Designs
Music	A World of Music	Elements of Music
	A World of Music	Musical Instructions

1

- **Social Studies**
- **History and Geography**

What Is a Globe?

Key Words

- **globe**
- **model**
- **continent**
- **grid**
- **imaginary line**
- **latitude**
- **longitude**
- **North Pole**
- **South Pole**

Look around your classroom. You can probably see a globe in it. What is a globe? A globe is a model of the earth that shows what the earth looks like.

A globe is a kind of map. It shows all of the land and water on the earth. You can turn a globe and see all seven continents and five oceans. But that is not all that a globe shows.

Look carefully at the globe. There are many lines on it. Some are horizontal lines while others are vertical lines. These lines on the grid are two sets of imaginary lines that circle the earth.

The horizontal lines that circle from east to west are lines of latitude. The vertical lines that circle from north to south are lines of longitude. The lines of longitude pass through the North Pole and the South Pole. When we know the latitude and longitude of a place, we know its exact location on the globe.

✓ A globe shows all of the land and water on the earth.

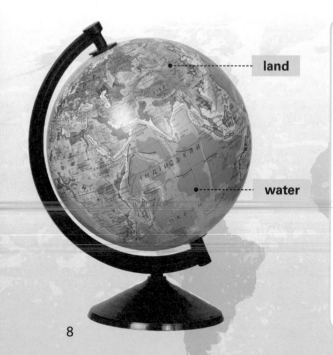

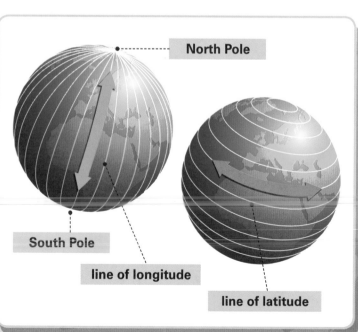

Main Idea and Details

1 **What is the passage mainly about?**

  a. The earth's continents and oceans.   **b.** The features of a globe.
  c. Lines of latitude and longitude.

2 **Lines of latitude are _____ lines.**

  a. horizontal   **b.** vertical   **c.** diagonal

3 **Why is knowing a place's latitude and longitude important?**

  a. It tells us how close to the North Pole it is.
  b. It tells us the name of the place.
  c. It tells us the place's exact location.

4 **What does imaginary mean?**

  a. Real.   **b.** Not real.   **c.** Colorful.

5 **Complete the sentences.**

  a. A globe is a _____ of the earth.
  b. Lines of longitude run from _____ to south.
  c. Lines of _____ run from east to west.

6 **Complete the outline.**

A Globe

What It Is	What It Shows	Latitude and Longitude
• A model of the ᵃ_____ • Shows what the earth looks like	• Land and water • All seven ᵇ_____ and five oceans	• Latitude = ᶜ_____ lines that circle from east to west • ᵈ_____ = vertical lines that circle from north to south

Vocabulary Builder

Write the correct word and the meaning in Chinese.

 **1** ▸ a pattern of straight lines that cross each other to form squares

_____

 **2** ▸ a model of the earth

_____

 **3** ▸ a horizontal line that circles from east to west on the globe

_____

 **4** ▸ a vertical line that circles from north to south on the globe

_____

Unit 02

Geography Skills
Understanding Hemispheres

Key Words

- geographer
- divide
- hemisphere
- hemi
- cover
- equator
- lie
- prime meridian

Geographers divide the earth into four different hemispheres. They are the Northern, Southern, Western, and Eastern hemispheres. The word "hemi" means "half." A hemisphere covers exactly one half of the earth.

The earth is divided into the Northern and Southern hemispheres by the equator. The equator is the line of latitude that lies in the middle of the earth. Above the equator is the Northern Hemisphere. Asia, Europe, and North America are in it. Below the equator is the Southern Hemisphere. It includes parts of Africa and South America. Australia and Antarctica are in it, too.

The earth is divided into the Eastern and Western hemispheres by the prime meridian. The prime meridian is a line of longitude that goes from the North Pole to the South Pole. It goes directly through Greenwich, England. North and South America are in the Western Hemisphere. Europe, Asia, Africa, Australia, and Antarctica are in the Eastern Hemisphere.

✓ The earth is divided into four different hemispheres.

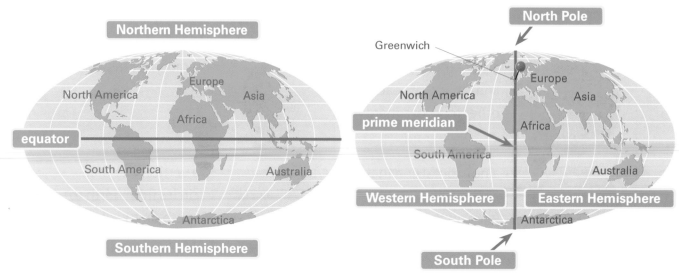

Main Idea and Details

1 **What is the main idea of the passage?**
   a. The word "hemi" means "half."
   b. There are many continents in the Northern Hemisphere.
   c. We can divide the earth into different hemispheres.

2 **Europe is in the** _____.
   a. Southern Hemisphere   **b.** Northern Hemisphere   **c.** Western Hemisphere

3 **What is the equator?**
   a. A line that runs next to the prime meridian.
   b. A line of latitude in the middle of the earth.
   c. A line of longitude from the North Pole to the South Pole.

4 **What does divided mean?**
   a. Stretched.   **b.** Showed.   **c.** Split.

5 **According to the passage, which statement is true?**
   a. North America is in the Eastern Hemisphere.
   b. Europe is in the Southern Hemisphere.
   c. The prime meridian goes from the North Pole to the South Pole.

6 **Complete the outline.**

Hemispheres

Northern Hemisphere	Southern Hemisphere	Western Hemisphere	Eastern Hemisphere
• Is north of the a _____ • Includes Asia, Europe, and North America	• Is south of the equator • Includes Australia, b _____, and parts of Africa and South America	• Is west of the prime meridian • Includes North and c _____ _____	• Is east of the prime meridian • Includes Europe, Africa, Asia, d _____, and Antarctica

Vocabulary Builder

Write the correct word and the meaning in Chinese.

1 ▶ to separate (something) into two or more parts or pieces

_____

2 ▶ to be located in a particular place

_____

3 ▶ an imaginary line that lies in the middle of the earth

_____

4 ▶ an imaginary line that goes from the North Pole to the South Pole

_____

The Environment of the West

Key Words

- touch
- coastline
- lush
- rugged
- extreme
- earthquake
- strike
- coast
- active volcano
- numerous
- fertile soil

The states in the West are all near the Pacific Ocean. They are California, Nevada, Oregon, and Washington. Alaska and Hawaii are in the western region, but they do not touch any other states.

The states in the West are known for their long coastlines along the Pacific, lush forests, hot deserts, and rugged mountains.

The West has a variety of climates. Nevada and California have many deserts. Death Valley, California, is one of the driest places on the planet. But there are also many places that get lots of rain. In fact, even rain forests are found in Oregon and Washington. The western climate sometimes can be very extreme. Earthquakes often strike along the Pacific coast. There are active volcanoes in Alaska, Hawaii, and Washington.

The West has numerous natural resources. There is plenty of fertile soil for farming. The forests provide much valuable wood throughout the country. The West is also a region of low valleys and tall mountains. The Cascade Range and Sierra Nevada Mountains are all located in the West.

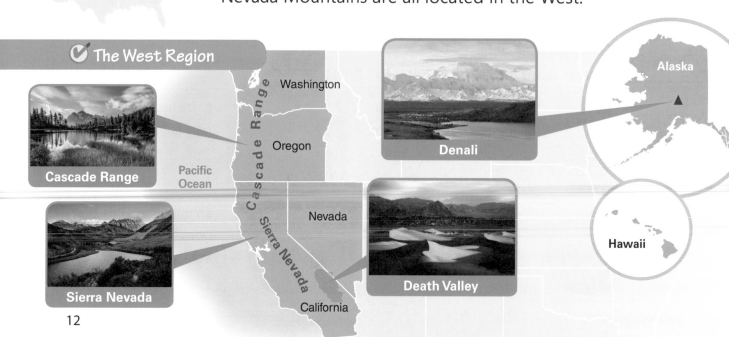

The West Region

Cascade Range

Washington

Oregon

Pacific Ocean

Cascade Range

Sierra Nevada

Nevada

California

Cascade Range

Sierra Nevada

Denali

Death Valley

Alaska

Hawaii

Main Idea and Details

1 **What is the main idea of the passage?**

   a. The West has a unique geography and different climates.

   b. Earthquakes and volcanoes are problems in the West.

   c. There are several major mountain ranges in the West.

2 **Death Valley is located in _____.**

   a. California   **b.** Alaska   **c.** Hawaii

3 **Which state in the West has active volcanoes?**

   a. California.   **b.** Alaska.   **c.** Oregon.

4 **What does lush mean?**

   a. Orange.   **b.** Green.   **c.** Brown.

5 **Answer the questions.**

   a. Which states are in the West? _____

   b. What often strikes along the Pacific coast? _____

   c. Where are some rain forests located? _____

6 **Complete the outline.**

The West

States	Climate	Geography
• California, Nevada, Oregon, Washington, Alaska, and a _____	• Nevada and California = many b _____ • Death Valley is very dry. • Many places get lots of rain.	• There are active volcanoes in Alaska, Hawaii, and Washington. • There is much c _____ soil for farming. • There are many lush d _____, low valleys, and rugged mountains.

Vocabulary Builder

Write the correct word and the meaning in Chinese.

 **1** ▸ having lots of green and healthy plants

_____

 **2** ▸ uneven and covered with rocks

_____

 **3** ▸ to happen suddenly and unexpectedly and cause damage

_____

 **4** ▸ an area of land beside an ocean

_____

Key Words

- carpenter
- hire
- mill
- flake
- discovery
- secret
- rush
- gold rush
- miner
- forty-niner
- empty handed
- population
- bustling

James Marshall was a carpenter who was hired at Sutter's Mill in California. In 1848, he was building a mill along the American River for John Sutter. One day, while working on the mill, Marshall found some flakes of a shiny metal in the river. He and John Sutter tried to keep this discovery a secret. However, rumors soon started to spread, and then everyone knew there was gold in California.

It took months for people in the East to hear the news. But, soon, thousands of people had moved to California. By 1849, more than 80,000 people had rushed to California. They were all looking for gold. This was the California Gold Rush. People called these gold miners "forty-niners" because they arrived in California in 1849. Some found gold and became rich. Others found nothing and left empty-handed.

During the early 1800s, the West was a quiet region with a small population. However, the discovery of gold changed the West into a land with bustling cities. The population also exploded, and California became a state in 1850.

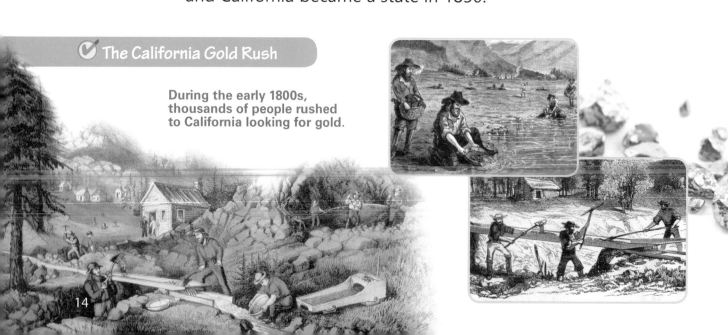

The California Gold Rush

During the early 1800s, thousands of people rushed to California looking for gold.

Main Idea and Details

1   What is the passage mainly about?

a. Who the first person to discover gold in California was.

b. How the California Gold Rush changed California.

c. When the California Gold Rush took place.

2   Where was gold first discovered?

a. At Sutter's Mill.   **b.** At Marshall's Mill.   **c.** At the Forty-Niners' Mill.

3   When did many people arrive in California to look for gold?

a. 1848.   b. 1849.   c. 1850.

4   What does hired mean?

a. Built.   **b.** Worked.   **c.** Employed.

5   Complete the sentences.

a. James Marshall tried to keep the discovery of gold a _____.

b. The people who were looking for gold were called _____.

c. In _____, California became a state.

6   Complete the outline.

The California Gold Rush

The Discovery of Gold	The Forty-Niners	Changes to California
• Was discovered by James Marshall at Sutter's Mill in 1848 • Tried to keep it a secret • ᵃ_____ soon started to spread.	• Were the people who went to California looking for gold in 1849 • Some became rich. • Others left ᵇ_____ handed.	• Had a small ᶜ_____ in the early 1800s • Became a land with bustling cities after gold was discovered • Became a ᵈ_____ in 1850

Vocabulary Builder

Write the correct word and the meaning in Chinese.

1 ▸ someone whose job is to dig coal, gold, etc. from the ground

_____

2 ▸ the process of finding something that was hidden; something that is found

_____

3 ▸ a sudden movement of people into an area where gold was discovered

_____

4 ▸ full of busy, noisy, and energetic people

_____

A

Complete the sentences with the words below.

Western	looks	pass through	circle
half	equator	horizontal	lies

1 A globe is a model of the earth that shows what the earth _____ like.

2 The _____ lines that circle from east to west are lines of latitude.

3 The vertical lines that _____ from north to south are lines of longitude.

4 The lines of longitude _____ _____ the North Pole and the South Pole.

5 A hemisphere covers exactly one _____ of the earth.

6 The earth is divided into the Northern and Southern hemispheres by the _____.

7 The equator is the line of latitude that _____ in the middle of the earth.

8 The earth is divided into the Eastern and _____ hemispheres by the prime meridian.

B

Complete the sentences with the words below.

discovery	secret	variety	hired
extreme	fertile	flakes	coastlines

1 The states in the West are known for their long _____ along the Pacific.

2 The West has a _____ of climates.

3 The western climate sometimes can be very _____.

4 There is plenty of _____ soil for farming in the West.

5 James Marshall was a carpenter who was _____ at Sutter's Mill in California.

6 One day, Marshall found some _____ of a shiny metal in the river.

7 He and John Sutter tried to keep this discovery a _____.

8 The _____ of gold changed the West into a land with bustling cities.

C

Write the correct word and the meaning in Chinese.

 ▸ a piece of information that is kept hidden from other people

_____

 ▸ a horizontal line that circles from east to west on the globe

_____

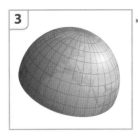 ▸ one half of the earth

_____

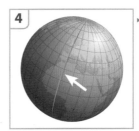 ▸ an imaginary line that goes from the North Pole to the South Pole

_____

 ▸ uneven and covered with rocks

_____

 ▸ a volcano that may erupt at any time

_____

D

Match each word with the correct definition and write the meaning in Chinese.

1 model   _____ ☐

2 line of longitude _____ ☐

3 geographer   _____ ☐

4 prime meridian   _____ ☐

5 carpenter   _____ ☐

6 lush   _____ ☐

7 extreme   _____ ☐

8 gold rush   _____ ☐

9 rush   _____ ☐

10 bustling   _____ ☐

a. to move or do very quickly

b. a small copy of something

c. very great in degree or intensity

d. having lots of green and healthy plants

e. full of busy, noisy, and energetic people

f. a person whose area of study is geography

g. a person whose job is making and repairing wooden things

h. an imaginary line that goes from the North Pole to the South Pole

i. a vertical line that circles from north to south on the globe

j. a sudden movement of people into an area where gold was discovered

The Environment of the Southwest

Key Words

- climate
- unusual
- landform
- geographical
- feature
- plateau
- canyon
- mesa
- butte
- flow through

The Southwest is famous for its sunny climate and unusual landforms. Arizona, New Mexico, Oklahoma, and Texas are the four states in the Southwest.

Much of the Southwest is hot and dry. So many parts of the land are covered by deserts. The Painted Desert and Sonoran Desert are located in Arizona.

But it still has many different geographical features. The Rocky Mountains run through the Southwest. There are also many plateaus, canyons, mesas, and buttes. The Colorado Plateau is the major plateau found in the Southwest. The area is famous for its canyons. The Grand Canyon is one of them.

While much of the land is dry, there are still some major rivers in the Southwest. The Colorado River flows through Arizona. It actually created the Grand Canyon. The Rio Grande River is another major river. It flows between Texas and Mexico.

The Southwest Region

Grand Canyon

Painted Desert

Colorado Plateau

Rocky Mountains

Colorado River

Arizona

Rocky Mountains

New Mexico

Oklahoma

Colorado River

Sonoran Desert

Texas

Mexico

Rio Grande River

Rio Grande River

Sonoran Desert

Main Idea and Details

1 **What is the passage mainly about?**

   a. Unusual landforms.

   b. A region in the United States.

   c. The Grand Canyon.

2 **There are many _____ in the Southwest.**

   a. forests   **b.** plains   **c.** deserts

3 **What is a river that flows through the Southwest?**

   a. The Colorado River.   **b.** The Arizona River.   **c.** The Texas River.

4 **What does climate mean?**

   a. Weather.   **b.** Rain.   **c.** Sun.

5 **Answer the questions.**

   a. What are the names of two deserts in Arizona? _____

   b. What mountains are in the Southwest? _____

   c. What are two major rivers in the Southwest? _____

6 **Complete the outline.**

```
                        The Southwest

   States          Climate and Landforms          Rivers

• Arizona,         • Sunny and dry            • Colorado River in Arizona
  New Mexico,      • b _____ like the Painted • Rio Grande River
  Oklahoma, and      Desert and the Sonoran Desert  d _____ Texas and
  a _____       • Many plateaus, canyons, mesas,  Mexico
                     and c _____
```

Vocabulary Builder

Write the correct word and the meaning in Chinese.

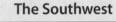 **1** ▸ relating to the natural features of a place

_____

2 ▸ a high, wide area of flat land that rises steeply above the land

_____

 **3** ▸ a hill with a flat top and steep sides in a flat area of land (usually narrower than a mesa)

_____

 **4** ▸ a small area of flat high land with steep sides (usually larger than a butte and smaller than a plateau)

_____

Key Words

- rich in
- mine
- petroleum
- nickname
- black gold
- thriving
- petrochemical industry
- high-technology industry
- aircraft

Although the Southwest gets little rainfall, it is rich in natural resources. Two of the most important resources are found beneath the ground. They are minerals and oil.

Minerals such as coal, copper, silver, and uranium are mined in Texas, Arizona, and New Mexico. Texas and Oklahoma are two of the largest producers of oil. Oil is a common name for petroleum. It is also nicknamed "black gold" since it is so valuable. "Black gold" has helped build the region's economy. The oil found in the Southwest is used throughout the United States.

Today, the states in the Southwest have thriving economies. Every year, more and more Americans move to the Southwest. The reason is that there are many different industries in the Southwest.

The oil industry continues to be a big business in the Southwest. The petrochemical industry is big there, too. Trade and high-technology industries, such as aircraft production, also help the Southwest grow.

✔ Minerals and oil have helped the Southwest grow.

oil = black gold

Arizona
copper silver
coal

New Mexico
silver
copper
coal

Oklahoma
oil

Texas
copper silver coal
oil

copper mine in Arizona

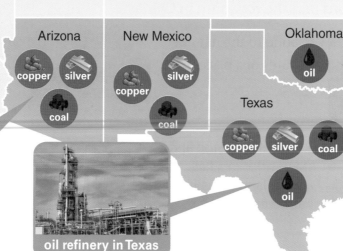
oil refinery in Texas

oil pump in Oklahoma

Main Idea and Details

1 **What is the main idea of the passage?**

a. People in the Southwest call oil "black gold."

b. Minerals and the oil industry are important in the Southwest.

c. There are many high-technology industries in the Southwest.

2 **Another name for oil is _____.**

a. copper　　　　　　**b.** uranium　　　　　　**c.** petroleum

3 **Which mineral do people mine in the Southwest?**

a. Silver.　　　　　　**b.** Gold.　　　　　　**c.** Iron.

4 **What does rich mean?**

a. Important.　　　　　　**b.** Wealthy.　　　　　　**c.** Unique.

5 **Complete the sentences.**

a. Many important resources in the Southwest are found under the _____.

b. Nowadays, many people are _____ to the Southwest.

c. Some high-technology companies in the Southwest produce _____.

6 **Complete the outline.**

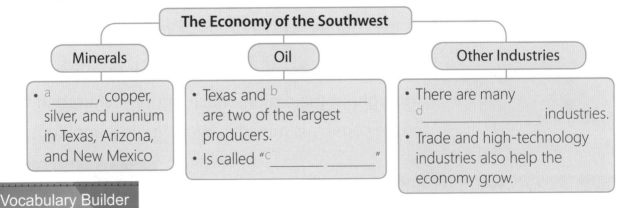

The Economy of the Southwest

Minerals	Oil	Other Industries
• ᵃ_____, copper, silver, and uranium in Texas, Arizona, and New Mexico	• Texas and ᵇ_____ are two of the largest producers. • Is called "ᶜ_____ _____"	• There are many ᵈ_____ industries. • Trade and high-technology industries also help the economy grow.

Vocabulary Builder

Write the correct word and the meaning in Chinese.

 ▸ oil; petroleum

_____

 ▸ to dig in the ground in order to get gold, coal, etc.

_____

 ▸ very successful

_____

 ▸ containing a large quantity of something

_____

The Environment of the Southeast

Key Words

- **agriculture**
- **heavy rainfall**
- **fertile soil**
- **a variety of**
- **crop**
- **growing season**
- **source**
- **wetland**
- **valuable**
- **coal**
- **mine**

One of the largest regions in the United States is the Southeast. It includes twelve states. They are Alabama, Arkansas, Florida, Georgia, Kentucky, Louisiana, Mississippi, North Carolina, South Carolina, Tennessee, Virginia, and West Virginia.

Agriculture is a large part of the region's economy. Because of its location, the Southeast has a warm climate for much of the year. The heavy rainfall and fertile soil there help farmers grow a variety of crops. Its long growing season also makes the Southeast a source of many fruits and vegetables.

The Southeast has many rivers, lakes, and wetlands. The Mississippi River flows through the western part of the Southeast. The Mississippi River has been at the center of travel and trade in the country for hundreds of years.

There are also many valuable natural resources throughout the region. Much of the coal used in the entire country is mined in West Virginia and Kentucky.

Mississippi River

✓ **The Southeast Region**

West Virginia
Kentucky
Virginia
Tennessee
North Carolina
Arkansas
South Carolina
Mississippi
Mississippi River
Georgia
Alabama
Louisiana
Florida

coal mine in West Virginia

A long growing season allows many crops to grow.

Main Idea and Details

1 What is the passage mainly about?

   a. The number of states in the Southeast.

   b. The economy and geography of the Southeast.

   c. The types of natural resources in the Southeast.

2 A major center of trade in the Southeast is _____.

   a. West Virginia and Kentucky   **b.** the Mississippi River   **c.** Alabama and Georgia

3 What is a natural resource that is mined in the Southeast?

   a. Gold.   **b.** Silver.   **c.** Coal.

4 What does agriculture mean?

   a. Crops.   **b.** Farming.   **c.** Growing.

5 According to the passage, which statement is true?

   a. There are twenty states in the Southeast.

   b. Most states in the Southeast get very little rain.

   c. Farmers in the Southeast grow many different crops.

6 Complete the outline.

The Southeast

States	Geography and Climate	Economy
• Alabama, Arkansas, Florida, Georgia, Kentucky, Louisiana, Mississippi, North Carolina, South Carolina, Tennessee, Virginia, and ᵃ_____ _____	• Has many rivers, lakes, and wetlands • ᵇ_____ River flows through it. • Has a warm climate • Gets heavy ᶜ_____	• Farmers grow a variety of crops, fruits, and vegetables. • Mine natural ᵈ_____ such as coal

Vocabulary Builder

Write the correct word and the meaning in Chinese.

1 ▸ the work, business, or study of farming

_____

2 ▸ the period of the year that is warm enough for plants to grow

_____

3 ▸ a plant such as corn that is grown by farmers and used as food

_____

4 ▸ land that has wet and spongy soil, such as marshes and swamps

_____

Key Words

- plantation
- cash crop
- cotton
- slave
- slavery
- illegal
- Civil War
- segregation
- Civil Rights Movement
- protest
- demand
- treatment
- Civil Rights Act
- guarantee

In the 1800s, most people in the Southeast farmed. There were many plantations. Plantation owners grew cash crops that they could sell to make money. Cotton was the most important cash crop.

Plantations required many workers, so many Southerners owned slaves. These slaves were black Africans. Their lives were very difficult.

Meanwhile, slavery was illegal in most Northern states. Many Northerners believed that slavery was wrong and should be ended. In the 1860s, the North and South fought the Civil War. The North won, and slavery became illegal.

However, most blacks in the South still did not have the same rights as white citizens. There was a lot of segregation. Blacks could not live together, work together, or even use the same restrooms with whites.

In the 1950s, the Civil Rights Movement began. Martin Luther King, Jr. became one of its leaders. He led protests demanding equal treatment for all people. Finally, in 1964, the Civil Rights Act was passed. It guaranteed that everyone would be treated equally.

Cotton Plantation

Cotton was an important cash crop in the South.

The Civil Rights Movement

Blacks demanded the same rights as whites.

24

Main Idea and Details

1 **What is the main idea of the passage?**

    a. Black Africans used to be slaves and work on plantations in the U.S.

    b. Martin Luther King, Jr. was a leader of the Civil Rights Movement.

    c. It took a long time for blacks and whites to become equal in the U.S.

2 **Many slaves worked on _____ in the Southeast.**

    a. cash crops   **b.** factories   **c.** plantations

3 **When was the Civil War?**

    a. The 1760s.   **b.** The 1860s.   **c.** The 1960s.

4 **What does guaranteed mean?**

    a. Promised.   **b.** Protected.   **c.** Guided.

5 **Answer the questions.**

    a. What was an important cash crop in the Southeast? _____

    b. Who fought the Civil War? _____

    c. When did the Civil Rights Movement begin? _____

6 **Complete the outline.**

The Civil Rights Movement

Slavery	Blacks in the South	The Civil Rights Act
• Plantations in the Southeast needed workers. • Used black African ᵃ_____ • Were freed after Civil War	• Did not have the same ᵇ_____ as whites • Were segregated • Could not live or work with ᶜ_____	• Civil Rights ᵈ_____ began in 1950s. • Martin Luther King, Jr. was a leader. • Civil Rights Act was ᵉ_____ in 1964.

Vocabulary Builder

Write the correct word and the meaning in Chinese.

1 ▸ the war in the United States between the North and the South, 1861–1865

_____

2 ▸ a strong complaint or disagreement

_____

3 ▸ the system of having slaves

_____

4 ▸ the policy of keeping people of different races, religions, etc., separate from each other

_____

Vocabulary **Review 2**

A Complete the sentences with the words below.

> plateau   nicknamed   thriving   climate
> major   located   rainfall   mined

1   The Southwest is famous for its sunny _____ and unusual landforms.

2   The Painted Desert and Sonoran Desert are _____ in Arizona.

3   The Colorado Plateau is the major _____ found in the Southwest.

4   While much of the land is dry, there are still some _____ rivers in the Southwest.

5   Although the Southwest gets little _____, it is rich in natural resources.

6   Minerals such as coal, copper, silver, and uranium are _____ in Texas, Arizona, and New Mexico.

7   Oil is also _____ "black gold" since it is so valuable.

8   Today, the states in the Southwest have _____ economies.

B Complete the sentences with the words below.

> plantation   flows   equally   location
> throughout   slaves   Civil War   growing

1   Because of its _____, the Southeast has a warm climate for much of the year.

2   Its long _____ season makes the Southeast a source of many fruits and vegetables.

3   The Mississippi River _____ through the western part of the Southeast.

4   There are many valuable natural resources _____ the Southeast region.

5   _____ owners grew cash crops that they could sell to make money.

6   Plantations required many workers, so many Southerners owned _____.

7   In the 1860s, the North and South fought the _____ _____.

8   The Civil Rights Act guaranteed that everyone would be treated _____.

26

C

Write the correct word and the meaning in Chinese.

 **1**
▸ a high, wide area of flat land that rises steeply above the land

_____

 **2**
▸ a deep, narrow valley with steep sides

_____

 **3**
▸ a hill with a flat top and steep sides in a flat area of land (usually narrower than a mesa)

_____

 **4**
▸ to dig in the ground in order to get gold, coal, etc.

_____

 **5**
▸ a large farm where crops such as cotton or sugarcane are grown

_____

 **6**
▸ a crop that is grown to be sold for money

_____

D

Match each word with the correct definition and write the meaning in Chinese.

1 landform _____ ☐

2 mine _____ ☐

3 thriving _____ ☐

4 aircraft _____ ☐

5 rainfall _____ ☐

6 fertile _____ ☐

7 crop _____ ☐

8 wetland _____ ☐

9 slavery _____ ☐

10 segregation _____ ☐

a. very successful

b. rich and productive

c. the system of having slaves

d. a plane or any vehicle that can fly

e. a plant such as corn that is grown by farmers and used as food

f. to dig in the ground in order to get gold, coal, etc.

g. the separation of a group of people from others because of race

h. land that has wet and spongy soil, such as marshes and swamps

i. a geographical feature that helps make up the earth's surface

j. the amount of rain that falls on an area in a particular time

Key Words

- subregion
- bay
- cape
- harbor
- trading center
- mountain chain
- mountain range
- distinct
- foliage
- well-known
- feature

The Northeast is divided into two subregions: New England and the Middle Atlantic States. The New England states are Maine, New Hampshire, Massachusetts, Vermont, Rhode Island, and Connecticut. The Middle Atlantic States are New York, Pennsylvania, New Jersey, Delaware, and Maryland.

Along the Atlantic coast, there are many bays, capes, and islands. Cape Cod, Massachusetts, is one of the most famous capes in the Northeast. The Atlantic Coastal Plain has many deep harbors. Cities with harbors can easily trade with other regions and countries. So, the Northeast cities, such as New York, Boston, and Philadelphia, have become important trading centers.

There are many mountain chains, too. The Appalachian Mountains are found in almost every state in the Northeast. The Appalachians are one of the oldest mountain ranges in the world.

The Northeastern states enjoy four distinct seasons. So they can be very hot in summer but very cold in winter. In fall, the colorful foliage is a well-known feature of the Northeast's forests.

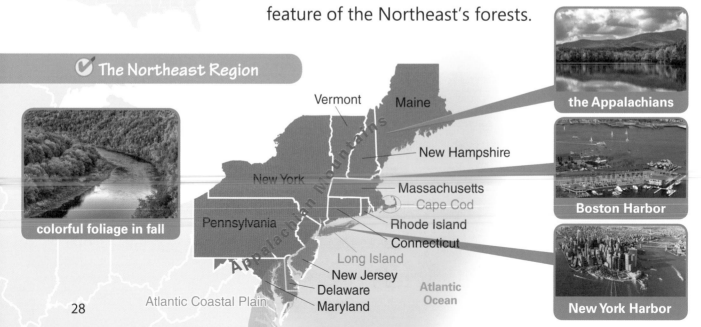

The Northeast Region

colorful foliage in fall

Vermont
Maine
New Hampshire
New York
Massachusetts
Cape Cod
Rhode Island
Connecticut
Pennsylvania
Long Island
New Jersey
Delaware
Maryland
Atlantic Coastal Plain
Appalachian Mountains
Atlantic Ocean

the Appalachians

Boston Harbor

New York Harbor

Main Idea and Details

1 **What is the passage mainly about?**
   a. Famous cities in the Northeast.   **b.** The geography of the Northeast.
   c. The fall foliage in the Northeast.

2 **An important trading center in the Northeast is _____.**
   a. Philadelphia   **b.** Detroit   **c.** Chicago

3 **What kind of mountain chain are the Appalachian Mountains?**
   a. An old mountain chain.   **b.** A high mountain chain.
   c. A dangerous mountain chain.

4 **What does distinct mean?**
   a. Colorful.   **b.** Unusual.   **c.** Separate.

5 **Complete the sentences.**
   a. There are two _____ in the Northeast.
   b. One of the most famous capes in the Northeast is _____ _____.
   c. There is a lot of colorful _____ in the forests in fall.

6 **Complete the outline.**

The Northeast

States
- New England = Maine, New Hampshire, Massachusetts, Vermont, Rhode Island, and Connecticut
- Middle Atlantic States = New York, Pennsylvania, New Jersey, Delaware, and ᵃ_____

Geography
- Has many bays, capes, islands, and deep ᵇ_____
- Has many mountain chains like the Appalachian Mountains

Climate
- Has four distinct ᶜ_____
- Is very hot in summer and very cold in winter
- Has colorful foliage in ᵈ_____

Vocabulary Builder

Write the correct word and the meaning in Chinese.

 ► a division of a region

 ► a mountain chain

 ► leaves

 ► a large piece of land that sticks out into the sea from the coast

Key Words

- settler
- Industrial Revolution
- replace
- hand tool
- expand
- spread
- manufacturing industry
- immigrant
- opportunity
- metropolitan area
- financial center
- import
- export

Many of the first settlers from Europe settled in the Northeast. Many were farmers. In the mid 1700s, most Americans lived and worked on farms. However, from the late 1700s to the mid 1800s, the Industrial Revolution changed the way people lived.

Machines replaced hand tools, and goods were produced faster. New industries were created, and the economy expanded. Factories soon became as important as farms.

As the Industrial Revolution spread across the country, the Northeast became the center of the country's manufacturing industry. All of the new factories and businesses needed many workers. So, more and more immigrants came to New York looking for new opportunities.

Based on size, the Northeast is the smallest area in the U.S. However, it is big in many ways. The Northeast has more metropolitan areas than any other region. Education is also very important in the Northeast. Excellent schools like Harvard, Yale, and MIT are there. New York City is the world's leading financial center. Also, the airports and ports all over the Northeast help import and export huge amounts of goods.

✔ The Industrial Revolution changed the way people lived forever.

Large-scale factories were built.

Goods were produced faster.

Many immigrants came to New York.

Main Idea and Details

1 **What is the main idea of the passage?**

    a. The Industrial Revolution took place in the Northeast.

    b. The Northeast is an important economic center in the U.S.

    c. Many excellent schools are located in the Northeast.

2 **Many _____ arrived in New York to look for new opportunities.**

    a. factories   **b.** financial centers   **c.** immigrants

3 **What changed the way many people lived?**

    a. The Industrial Revolution.   **b.** Harvard, Yale, and MIT.   **c.** Factories and farms.

4 **What does spread mean?**

    a. Expanded.   **b.** Replaced.   **c.** Exported.

5 **According to the passage, which statement is true?**

    a. The Industrial Revolution started in the early 1700s.

    b. People built many factories in the Northeast.

    c. The Northeast is the biggest region in the United States.

6 **Complete the outline.**

The Northeast and Its Industries

The Industrial Revolution	Manufacturing Industry	Other Industries
• Changed the ᵃ_____ people lived • Machines replaced hand tools. • Goods were produced faster.	• Northeast was the center of the U.S. ᵇ_____ industry. • Factories needed workers. • Used many immigrants	• There are many excellent schools. • New York City = leading ᶜ_____ center • Airports and ports import and ᵈ_____ many goods.

Vocabulary Builder

Write the correct word and the meaning in Chinese.

1 ▸ the revolution of machines that brought about large-scale factory production

_____

2 ▸ any tool or device designed for manual operation

_____

3 ▸ an area of population usually with a central city and surrounding suburbs

_____

4 ▸ the practice or business of selling goods to another country

_____

Key Words

- landform
- interior
- plain
- mighty
- breadbasket
- countless
- raise
- livestock
- automobile
- manufacturer

The Midwest region is made up of 12 states. They are Ohio, Indiana, Michigan, Wisconsin, Illinois, Minnesota, Iowa, Missouri, North Dakota, South Dakota, Nebraska, and Kansas.

The Midwest is made up of low, flat lands. The major landforms are the two interior plains: the Central Plains and the Great Plains. Also, three important rivers run through it. They are the mighty Mississippi River, the Ohio River, and the Missouri River. The Great Lakes are also in the Midwest.

The Midwest has two major industries: farming and manufacturing. The Midwest is called the "breadbasket of America." It has countless fields of wheat, corn, and other crops. Also, many Midwestern farmers raise pigs, cows, and other livestock. Much of America's food comes from the Midwest.

The Midwest is also a manufacturing center. Henry Ford started building cars in Detroit, Michigan. Detroit quickly became the automobile center of the world. Several large car manufacturers have factories there. There are also many other industries all throughout the Midwest.

The Midwest Region

Missouri River

Great Plains

North Dakota

Minnesota

South Dakota

Missouri River

Wisconsin

Michigan

Great Lakes

Lake Superior

Nebraska

Iowa

Mississippi River

Kansas

Illinois

Indiana

Ohio

Ohio River

Missouri

Great Plains

Detroit, the automobile center of the world

Main Idea and Details

1 **What is the passage mainly about?**

    a. The states in the Midwest.   **b.** The rivers and plains in the Midwest.

    c. The land and industries in the Midwest.

2 **Henry Ford built cars in _____.**

    a. Detroit   **b.** Chicago   **c.** Ohio

3 **Why is the Midwest called the "breadbasket of America"?**

    a. Because it raises livestock.   **b.** Because it builds cars.

    c. Because it provides much of the America's food.

4 **What does automobile mean?**

    a. Bike.   **b.** Car.   **c.** Factory.

5 **According to the passage, which statement is true?**

    a. There are three important rivers in the Midwest.

    b. Farmers in the Midwest only grow corn.

    c. Companies in Detroit build many airplanes.

6 **Complete the outline.**

The Midwest

States
- Ohio, Indiana, a _____, Wisconsin, Illinois, Minnesota, Iowa, Missouri, North Dakota, South Dakota, Nebraska, and Kansas

Geography
- Has low, flat lands
- The Central b _____ and the Great Plains are there.
- The Mississippi, Ohio, and Missouri rivers are there.
- The Great c _____ are there.

Economy
- Farming = raise crops and livestock
- The "breadbasket of America"
- Many d _____ industries are there.
- Detroit = automobile center of the world

Vocabulary Builder

Write the correct word and the meaning in Chinese.

 ▸ located on the inside of something

_____

2 ▸ a region that provides a lot of food for a country

_____

 ▸ to keep and take care of animals

_____

 ▸ animals that are kept on a farm

_____

Key Words

- majestic
- run through
- Continental Divide
- peak
- enormous
- inland
- salt water
- mining
- outdoor recreation
- rafting
- attract
- population

Idaho, Montana, Wyoming, Colorado, and Utah are the five states in the Mountain States region.

The Mountain States are covered with mountains. The majestic Rocky Mountains run through them. The Continental Divide runs north to south along the peaks of the Rockies. These states also have many rivers and enormous forests. Great Salt Lake is located in northern Utah. It is the largest inland body of salt water in the Western Hemisphere.

Mining is one of the most important industries in the Mountain States. The Rocky Mountains provide plenty of metal and mineral resources, such as copper and natural gas.

Tourism is another important industry in the Mountain States. Outdoor recreation, such as skiing, mountain climbing, and rafting, attracts thousands of tourists every year.

The population of the Mountain States is quite low. Few cities have populations greater than 50,000. Denver and Salt Lake City are the region's largest cities.

The Mountain States

Great Salt Lake

Montana

Idaho

Wyoming

Denver

Rocky Mountains

Great Salt Lake

Utah

Colorado

Continental Divide

Salt Lake City

Tourists enjoy a lot of outdoor recreation.

rafting

skiing

mountain climbing

34

Main Idea and Details

1 **What is the passage mainly about?**
   a. The populations of the Mountain States.
   b. The characteristics of the Mountain States.
   c. The geography of the Mountain States.

2 **Great Salt Lake is a large saltwater lake in _____.**
   a. Idaho   **b.** Wyoming   **c.** Utah

3 **Why do thousands of people visit the Mountain States every year?**
   a. To do outdoor recreation.   **b.** To mine the land.   **c.** To visit national parks.

4 **What does majestic mean?**
   a. Magnifying.   **b.** Magnificent.   **c.** Enormous.

5 **Complete the sentences.**
   a. The Continental Divide is located in the _____ Mountains.
   b. _____ is an important industry in the Mountain States.
   c. There are few big _____ in the Mountain States.

6 **Complete the outline.**

The Mountain States

States
- Idaho, Montana, Wyoming, Colorado, and a _____

Geography
- Are covered with mountains
- Rocky Mountains are there.
- The b _____ Divide is there.
- Have many rivers and enormous forests

Economy
- Mining c _____ and mineral resources like copper and natural gas
- Thousands visit for outdoor d _____

Vocabulary Builder

Write the correct word and the meaning in Chinese.

▸ the pointed top of a mountain; a tall mountain with a pointed or narrow top

_____

▸ the main series of mountain ridges in North America that form a watershed

_____

▸ an activity that you do for fun, such as skiing and rafting

_____

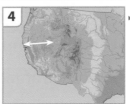
▸ in the middle of a country; away from the coast

_____

Vocabulary **Review 3**

A

Complete the sentences with the words below.

| harbors | subregions | along | Appalachians |
| distinct | replaced | Industrial | metropolitan |

1   The Northeast is divided into two _____ : New England and the Middle Atlantic States.

2   _____ the Atlantic coast, there are many bays, capes, and islands.

3   Cities with _____ can easily trade with other regions and countries.

4   The _____ are one of the oldest mountain ranges in the world.

5   The Northeastern states enjoy four _____ seasons.

6   The _____ Revolution changed the way people lived.

7   Machines _____ hand tools, and goods were produced faster.

8   The Northeast has more _____ areas than any other region.

B

Complete the sentences with the words below.

| manufacturing | outdoor | became | raise |
| made up | industries | inland | runs |

1   The Midwest region is _____ _____ of 12 states.

2   The Midwest has two major industries: farming and _____.

3   Many Midwestern farmers _____ pigs, cows, and other livestock.

4   Detroit quickly _____ the automobile center of the world.

5   The Continental Divide _____ north to south along the peaks of the Rockies.

6   Great Salt Lake is the largest _____ body of salt water in the Western Hemisphere.

7   Mining is one of the most important _____ in the Mountain States.

8   _____ recreation attracts thousands of tourists every year.

C

Write the correct word and the meaning in Chinese.

1  ▸ to buy a product from another country and bring it to your country

_____

2  ▸ a mountain chain

_____

3  ▸ leaves

_____

4  ▸ any tool or device designed for manual operation

_____

5  ▸ animals that are kept on a farm

_____

6  ▸ large and impressively beautiful

_____

D

Match each word with the correct definition and write the meaning in Chinese.

1 well-known _____ ☐

2 Industrial Revolution _____ ☐

3 replace _____ ☐

4 financial _____ ☐

5 mighty _____ ☐

6 breadbasket _____ ☐

7 countless _____ ☐

8 peak _____ ☐

9 mining _____ ☐

10 attract _____ ☐

a. to take the place of

b. very large or powerful

c. known by a lot of people; famous

d. too many to be counted; uncountable

e. to make someone interested in something

f. a region that provides a lot of food for a country

g. relating to money or the management of money

h. the top of a mountain

i. the industry of digging minerals from the ground; the action of digging

j. the revolution of machines that brought about large-scale factory production

Wrap-Up Test 1

A

Write the correct word for each sentence.

> metropolitan   nicknamed   landforms   globe   longitude
> hemispheres   Revolution   growing   Rockies   cash crops

1   A _____ is a model of the earth that shows what the earth looks like.

2   The lines of _____ pass through the North Pole and the South Pole.

3   The earth is divided into the Northern and Southern _____ by the equator.

4   The Southwest is famous for its sunny climate and unusual _____.

5   Oil is also _____ "black gold" since it is so valuable.

6   Its long _____ season makes the Southeast a source of many fruits and vegetables.

7   Plantation owners grew _____ _____ that they could sell to make money.

8   The Northeast has more _____ areas than any other region.

9   The Industrial _____ changed the way people lived.

10   The Continental Divide runs north to south along the peaks of the _____.

B

Write the meanings of the words in Chinese.

1	line of latitude		16	rainfall
2	hemisphere		17	fertile
3	equator		18	crop
4	line of longitude		19	wetland
5	prime meridian		20	slavery
6	landform		21	foliage
7	plateau		22	Industrial Revolution
8	petroleum		23	replace
9	thriving		24	financial
10	mesa		25	lush
11	plantation		26	extreme
12	cash crop		27	bustling
13	cape		28	rugged
14	mountain range		29	metropolitan
15	segregation		30	distinct

2

How Do Animals Grow?

Every animal has a life cycle. Just as there are many different kinds of animals, there are many kinds of life cycles.

Almost all animals come from fertilized eggs. Many birds lay eggs in nests. Fish and amphibians lay eggs in the water. Reptiles also lay eggs. They hatch from eggs outside a female's body. After hatching, some animals, such as frogs and insects, go through complete body changes before they become adults.

Mammals begin their lives inside their mothers. They develop from fertilized eggs inside their mothers' bodies. They are born live. When they are born, they are tiny but look a lot like the adults. As they grow, they get larger, and their faces change. However, they do not go through other major changes. This kind of growth is called direct development.

Animals also develop at different rates. A fruit fly becomes an adult in about 10 days. A dog becomes an adult at about three years of age.

Key Words

- life cycle
- fertilized egg
- lay
- nest
- amphibian
- reptile
- hatch
- go through
- mammal
- develop
- direct development

✔ Animals develop in different life cycles.

▶ **Some go through complete body changes.**

▶ **Some go through direct development.**

Main Idea and Details

1   What is the main idea of the passage?

a. Some animals die after a few days.   **b.** Many animals lay eggs.

c. Every animal has a life cycle.

2   Animals such as _____ may go through complete body changes.

a. dogs   **b.** frogs   **c.** birds

3   Which kinds of animals are born live?

a. Mammals.   **b.** Reptiles.   **c.** Birds.

4   What does develop mean?

a. Go through.   **b.** Hatch.   **c.** Grow.

5   Complete the sentences.

a. Birds usually lay their eggs in _____.

b. Mammals' faces _____ as they grow older.

c. Fruit flies become adults after around _____ days.

6   Complete the outline.

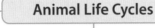

```
                          ┌─────────────────────┐
                          │  Animal Life Cycles │
                          └─────────────────────┘
```

Eggs	Live Births	Rates of Development
• Are laid by birds, fish, reptiles, and ª_____ • Hatch outside females' bodies • May go through ᵇ_____ body changes	• Are done by mammals • Begin lives in mothers' bodies • Are born ᶜ_____ • Are direct development	• Are all different • Fruit fly = 10 days to become an ᵈ_____ • Dog = 3 years to become an adult

Vocabulary Builder

Write the correct word and the meaning in Chinese.

 ▸ all of the stages an organism goes through

_____

 ▸ to produce an egg outside of the body

_____

 ▸ to come out of an egg by breaking the shell

_____

 ▸ development without going through major changes

_____

A World of Animals
What Is Metamorphosis?

Key Words

- undergo
- metamorphosis
- body form
- moth
- stage
- caterpillar
- larva
- prepare for
- cocoon
- shell
- spin
- thread
- pupa

Animals go through changes as they live and grow. Some animals, such as fish and people, just get larger as they grow older. However, some animals undergo big life cycle changes called metamorphosis.

Metamorphosis means a major change in the body form of an animal. Butterflies and moths undergo metamorphosis. Most amphibians, such as frogs, also go through metamorphosis.

There are four stages in complete metamorphosis. Let's look closely at the metamorphosis of a butterfly.

First, a butterfly lays a fertilized egg. In the second stage, a tiny caterpillar, or larva, hatches from the egg. The caterpillar begins eating and growing to prepare for the next stage. In the third stage, it forms a cocoon. This is a hard shell that the caterpillar makes by spinning threads around itself so that it becomes a pupa. Inside the cocoon, it undergoes a metamorphosis. At last, in the fourth stage, the adult butterfly comes out of the cocoon.

The Metamorphosis of a Butterfly

Stage 1 egg

Stage 2 caterpillar

Stage 3 pupa

Stage 4 adult butterfly

1 **What is the passage mainly about?**

a. How some animals undergo body changes.

b. Why butterflies undergo metamorphosis.

c. Which animals must change their bodies.

2 **There are _____ stages in the metamorphosis of a butterfly.**

a. four   **b.** five   **c.** six

3 **What is another name for a cocoon?**

a. Larva.   **b.** Pupa.   **c.** Egg.

4 **What does undergo mean?**

a. Create.   **b.** Go through.   **c.** Complete.

5 **According to the passage, which statement is true?**

a. The third stage in a butterfly's life is the adult stage.

b. Most butterflies never undergo metamorphosis.

c. A large number of amphibians go through metamorphosis.

6 **Complete the outline.**

```
                    Metamorphosis

      Some Animals              Four Stages of Butterflies

• a_____ and moths       • Lays an egg
  undergo it.                  • b_____ from an egg
• Most amphibians undergo it.  • The caterpillar, or larva, begins eating a lot.
                               • Makes a cocoon and changes as a c_____
                               • Emerges from the d_____ as an adult
```

Write the correct word and the meaning in Chinese.

 ▸ complete body changes of an animal during its life cycle

_____

 ▸ a very young form of an insect that looks like a worm

_____

 ▸ a hard shell that a caterpillar makes by spinning threads around itself

_____

 ▸ an insect such as a moth while it is changing inside a cocoon

_____

How Do Animals Respond to Changes?

Environments often change. Animals respond to changes in their environment in different ways.

Animals often rely on their instincts. Instinct is something animals are born with. For instance, they might realize which animals are dangerous and which ones are not. Also, a spider knows how to spin a web to catch food.

Many animals have adapted to winter by migrating or hibernating. When the weather gets cold, some animals migrate to warmer places in search of food. Some animals, like bears, find places to hibernate. Since its body is barely working, a hibernating animal does not need much energy, so it does not need to eat during the winter. Migration and hibernation are both instinctive behaviors.

Some animals also have learned behaviors. Mammal mothers usually teach their young learned behaviors. They teach their young how to get food and how to protect themselves. Bear cubs learn to climb trees at about six months. Most human behavior is learned.

Key Words

- respond
- rely on
- instinct
- born with
- spin a web
- adapt to
- migrate
- hibernate
- in search of
- barely
- instinctive behavior
- learned behavior

✔ Adaptations in Different Environments

instinctive behavior

migration

hibernation

learned behavior

climbing trees

getting food

Main Idea and Details

1 **What is the main idea of the passage?**
   a. Most animals rely only on their instincts.
   b. Instinctive behavior is more common than learned behavior.
   c. There are many ways for animals to respond to changes.

2 **One form of instinctive behavior is** _____.
   a. hibernating during winter   **b.** climbing a tree   **c.** getting food

3 **How do animals get instincts?**
   a. Their parents teach instincts to them.
   b. They are born with them.
   c. They learn them by observing other animals.

4 **What does rely on mean?**
   a. Respond to.   **b.** Depend on.   **c.** Born with.

5 **Answer the questions.**
   a. What kind of behavior is a spider spinning a web? _____
   b. Why do some animals migrate? _____
   c. What is an animal that hibernates? _____

6 **Complete the outline.**

Animal Adaptations

Instinctive Behavior

- Animals are ª_____ with it.
- Spiders know how to spin webs.
- Migrate to warm lands in ᵇ_____ of food
- Hibernate during winter so do not need to eat

Learned Behavior

- Are taught by mammal mothers to their ᶜ_____
- Learn how to get food and to ᵈ_____ themselves
- Bear cubs learn to climb trees.
- Most human behavior is learned.

Vocabulary Builder

Write the correct word and the meaning in Chinese.

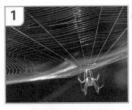 **1** ▸ a natural ability animals are born with

_____

 **2** ▸ to travel to another place for warmer weather at a particular time of the year

_____

 **3** ▸ a behavior taught by mothers or older animals

_____

 **4** ▸ to sleep all the time during the winter

_____

Adaptation
Animal Adaptations for Survival

Animals have various adaptations that help them survive. An adaptation might be a body part or behavior that an organism gets from its parents.

Frogs and lizards have long tongues that help them catch insects. Lions have great speed, strength, and sharp claws and teeth to hunt their food.

Many animals have body colors or shapes that match their surroundings. Camouflage is a good example. Animals in snowy areas often have white fur. Animals in forests often have brown fur. Some animals, like chameleons, can even change colors frequently to match their environment. When these animals stay still, a predator may not see them.

Some animals use mimicry to avoid being eaten by other animals. Mimicry is looking like another organism or object. The stonefish looks like a stone. The wings of the gray butterfly have spots that look like eyes of an owl. The snake mimic caterpillar looks like a real snake.

Key Words

- adaptation
- survive
- organism
- tongue
- claw
- match
- surroundings
- camouflage
- chameleon
- predator
- mimicry
- avoid
- stonefish
- snake mimic caterpillar

✔ Animal Adaptations and Defense Methods

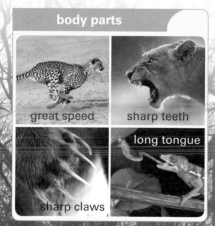

body parts

great speed

sharp teeth

long tongue

sharp claws

camouflage

chameleon

mimicry

▶ owl butterfly

▾ snake mimic caterpillar

stonefish

1   What is the passage mainly about?

    a. Some animals that use mimicry to survive.

    b. Different methods animals use to survive.

    c. The similarities between camouflage and mimicry.

2   Lions have both sharp _____ and teeth.

    a. legs   **b.** claws   **c.** tails

3   What does the gray butterfly use to be protected?

    a. Body color.   **b.** Camouflage.   **c.** Mimicry.

4   What does avoid mean?

    a. Keep from.   **b.** Stay up.   **c.** Match.

5   Complete the sentences.

    a. A frog uses its long _____ to catch insects.

    b. Animals with body colors that match their surroundings use _____.

    c. The stonefish uses _____ to look like a stone.

6   Complete the outline.

Animal Adaptations

Body Parts	Camouflage	Mimicry
• Frogs and lizards = long ^{a}_____ to catch insects • Lions = great speed, strength, and sharp claws and teeth to catch food	• Body ^{b}_____ or shape that matches surroundings • White animals in ^{c}_____ areas • Brown animals in forests • Chameleons	• Looking like another organism • Stonefish = looks like stone • Gray ^{d}_____ = has spots that look like eyes of an owl • Snake mimic caterpillar = looks like a ^{e}_____

Write the correct word and the meaning in Chinese.

▸ a body part or behavior that helps an organism survive

_____

▸ hiding something by making it look like the things around it

_____

▸ an animal that kills and eats other animals

_____

▸ looking like another organism

_____

A

Complete the sentences with the words below.

fertilized	go through	hatches	rates
mammals	metamorphosis	butterfly	stages

1   Almost all animals come from _____ eggs.

2   Some animals _____ _____ complete body changes before they become adults.

3   _____ begin their lives inside their mothers.

4   Animals also develop at different _____.

5   Some animals undergo big life cycle changes called _____.

6   There are four _____ in complete metamorphosis.

7   In the second stage, a tiny caterpillar, or larva, _____ from the egg.

8   At last, in the fourth stage, the adult _____ comes out of the cocoon.

B

Complete the sentences with the words below.

organism	respond	instinctive	adapted
behaviors	avoid	surroundings	tongues

1   Animals _____ to changes in their environment in different ways.

2   Many animals have _____ to winter by migrating or hibernating.

3   Migration and hibernation are both _____ behaviors.

4   Some animals also have learned _____.

5   An adaptation might be a body part or behavior that an _____ gets from its parents.

6   Frogs and lizards have long _____ that help them catch insects.

7   Many animals have body colors or shapes that match their _____.

8   Some animals use mimicry to _____ being eaten by other animals.

C **Write the correct word and the meaning in Chinese.**

1  ▸ all of the stages an organism goes through

_____

2  ▸ a natural ability animals are born with

_____

3  ▸ complete body changes of an animal during its life cycle

_____

4  ▸ a small long thin insect with many legs that develops into a butterfly or moth

_____

5 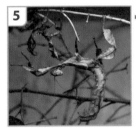 ▸ looking like another organism

_____

6  ▸ hiding something by making it look like the things around it

_____

D **Match each word with the correct definition and write the meaning in Chinese.**

1 fertilized egg _____ ☐

2 go through _____ ☐

3 spin thread _____ ☐

4 instinct _____ ☐

5 behavior _____ ☐

6 learned behavior _____ ☐

7 hibernate _____ ☐

8 adaptation _____ ☐

9 chameleon _____ ☐

10 mimicry _____ ☐

a. to experience; to undergo

b. looking like another organism

c. to sleep all the time during the winter

d. the way that an animal does things

e. a natural ability animals are born with

f. a behavior taught by mothers or older animals

g. a body part or behavior that helps an organism survive

h. to make a cocoon from the thread silkworms and others produce

i. a kind of lizard whose skin changes color to match its surroundings

j. the initial cell formed when a new organism is produced by sexual reproduction

What Changes Earth's Surface?

Key Words

- **weathering**
- **break down**
- **rushing water**
- **weather**
- **chemical**
- **erosion**
- **weathered**
- **carry away**
- **typically**
- **glacier**
- **blow away**

Earth's surface is changing all the time. Some changes are very slow. Some changes happen very quickly.

One kind of change is caused by weathering. Weathering is the process by which large rocks are broken down into small pieces for many years. Weathering can happen in many ways. Rushing water and strong winds can weather rocks. Changing temperatures and some chemicals can also weather rocks. Usually, weathering takes a very long time to occur.

Erosion happens after weathering. It occurs when weathered rocks or soil are carried away to other places. Typically, wind, water, and glaciers cause erosion. Like weathering, erosion is often a slow process. For example, it took the Colorado River millions of years to make the Grand Canyon. This is water erosion. Wind erosion can blow away valuable soil and make deserts. A glacier is a huge mass of moving ice. It moves rocks and other things in its path wherever it goes.

Slow Changes to Earth's Surface

weathering	erosion

water erosion   wind erosion   glacier erosion

1 **What is the passage mainly about?**

   a. How erosion can take place.

   b. What can change Earth's surface.

   c. Why weathering is important.

2 **Erosion occurs when _____ rocks are carried away to other places.**

   a. weathered   **b.** eroded   **c.** large

3 **How long did it take the Colorado River to make the Grand Canyon?**

   a. Hundreds of years.   **b.** Thousands of years.   **c.** Millions of years.

4 **What does Typically mean?**

   a. Quickly.   **b.** Usually.   **c.** Smoothly.

5 **According to the passage, which statement is true?**

   a. Weathering happens after erosion.

   b. The Grand Canyon was created by weathering.

   c. Weathering is caused by water, wind, and changing temperatures.

6 **Complete the outline.**

Changes to Earth's Surface

Weathering

- Is the ᵃ_____ down of large rocks into small pieces
- Can be caused by rushing water, strong winds, temperature changes, and ᵇ_____
- Often takes a long time to occur

Erosion

- Is the carrying away of ᶜ_____ rocks and soil
- Can be caused by wind, water, and glaciers
- Is a slow ᵈ_____

Write the correct word and the meaning in Chinese.

 **1** ▸ the process of the carrying away of weathered rocks and soil

_____

 **2** ▸ the process of the breaking down of large rocks into small pieces

_____

 **3** ▸ a very large area of ice that moves slowly down a slope or valley or over a wide area of land

_____

 **4** ▸ a substance (such as an element or compound) that is made by a chemical process

_____

2
Science

Fast Changes to Earth's Surface

Key Words

- earthquake
- volcano
- violent
- shaking
- sudden
- crust
- collapse
- route
- erupt
- lava
- build up
- underwater
- windstorm

Weathering and erosion usually take thousands of years to change Earth's surface. However, earthquakes, volcanoes, and other violent weathers can change Earth's surface quickly.

An earthquake is the shaking of Earth's surface caused by the sudden movement of rock in the crust. Earthquakes can cause great changes to the land. They can cause land to fall or rise. They can collapse mountains and even change the routes that rivers and streams follow.

Volcanoes can also instantly change Earth's surface. When a volcano erupts, lava and other materials flow onto Earth's surface. These materials build up to form a mountain. Many underwater volcanoes can even create islands in the middle of Earth's oceans.

Hurricanes, tornadoes, and floods can also change Earth's surface quickly. Hurricanes cause strong winds and heavy rains. Tornadoes are powerful windstorms that destroy most things in their paths. Floods carry away rocks and soil. These violent types of weather can change the land in just a few minutes or hours.

Fast Changes to Earth's Surface

earthquake

volcano

violent weather

lava dome

volcanic rock

Main Idea and Details

1 **What is the main idea of the passage?**
  a. Earthquakes can make rivers and streams change their routes.
  b. Volcanoes and hurricanes are two powerful forces of nature.
  c. Some forces of nature can quickly change Earth's surface.

2 **A powerful windstorm is called a _____ .**
  a. flood   **b.** volcano   **c.** tornado

3 **What happens when a volcano erupts?**
  a. Rocks and soil get carried away.
  b. Lava and other materials flow onto Earth's surface.
  c. Mountains collapse, and rivers and streams change their routes.

4 **What does collapse mean?**
  a. Build.   **b.** Destroy.   **c.** Move.

5 **Answer the questions.**
  a. What is an earthquake? _____
  b. What can underwater volcanoes do? _____
  c. How can floods change Earth's surface? _____

6 **Complete the outline.**

Fast Changes on Land

Earthquakes	Volcanoes	Hurricanes, Tornadoes, and Floods
• Are the sudden shaking of Earth's surface • Can cause land to ^a_____ or fall • Can collapse mountains • Can change the routes rivers and streams follow	• Cause ^b_____ and other materials to flow onto Earth's surface • Form mountains • Can create islands in the middle of oceans	• ^c_____ = strong winds and heavy rains • Tornadoes = powerful windstorms that destroy many things • ^d_____ = carry away rocks and soil

Vocabulary Builder

Write the correct word and the meaning in Chinese.

1 ► to break apart and fall down suddenly

_____

2 ► melted rock from a volcano

_____

3 ► a way from one place to another

_____

4 ► to happen suddenly; to spew; to send out into the sky

_____

Our Solar System

Key Words

- solar system
- orbit
- planet
- moon
- asteroid
- inner planet
- outer planet
- farther away
- rocky
- gas giant
- be surrounded by
- ring
- asteroid belt

The solar system is made up of the sun and all the objects that orbit it. This includes planets, moons, and asteroids. The sun is the largest object in our solar system.

The planets are divided into two groups: the inner planets and the outer planets. The inner planets are the four planets closest to the sun: Mercury, Venus, Earth, and Mars. The outer planets are Jupiter, Saturn, Uranus, and Neptune. They are farther away from the sun.

The inner planets all have rocky surfaces. They are smaller than the outer planets. None of the inner planets has more than two moons.

The outer planets are all huge and mostly made up of gases. They are often called gas giants. The outer planets all have many moons. They are also surrounded by rings that are made of dust, ice, or rock.

The asteroid belt separates the inner planets from the outer planets. It lies between Jupiter and Mars.

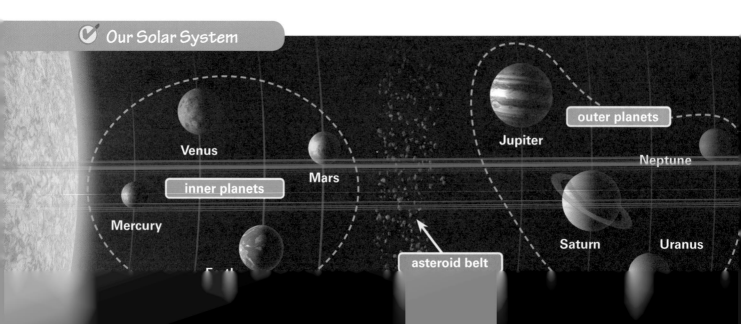

Our Solar System

Venus

Mars

inner planets

Mercury

asteroid belt

Jupiter

outer planets

Neptune

Saturn

Uranus

Main Idea and Details

1 **What is the main idea of the passage?**
  a. The solar system has several different planets in it.
  b. The outer planets are larger than the inner planets.
  c. There are two main groups of planets in the solar system.

2 **The four outer planets are known as** _____.
  a. gas giants   **b.** the asteroid belt   **c.** Mercury, Venus, Earth, and Mars

3 **Where is the asteroid belt?**
  a. Between Mars and Earth.   **b.** Between Jupiter and Saturn.
  c. Between Mars and Jupiter.

4 **What does orbit mean?**
  a. Move into.   **b.** Move around.   **c.** Move under.

5 **Answer the questions.**
  a. What are the four inner planets? _____
  b. What are the characteristics of the inner planets? _____
  c. What are the four outer planets? _____

6 **Complete the outline.**

The Solar System

The Inner Planets

- Mercury, Venus, ᵃ_____, and Mars
- Are the closest planets to the sun
- Have rocky surfaces
- Are smaller than the outer planets
- Have no more than two ᵇ_____

The Outer Planets

- Jupiter, Saturn, Uranus, and Neptune
- Are the farthest planets from the sun
- Are huge
- Are called ᶜ_____ _____
- Have many moons
- Are surrounded by ᵈ_____

Vocabulary Builder

Write the correct word and the meaning in Chinese.

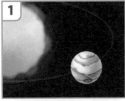
1 ▸ a large object that orbits the sun
_____

2 ▸ to travel around something in a curved path
_____

3 ▸ any of the planets whose orbits lie beyond the asteroid belt
_____

4 ▸ the belt of small objects between Mars and Jupiter
_____

The Sun and Other Stars

Key Words

- **celestial object**
- **comet**
- **mixture**
- **turn into**
- **tail**
- **constellation**
- **galaxy**
- **contain**
- **edge**
- **Milky Way Galaxy**

Our solar system has many celestial objects other than planets orbiting the sun. Two types of these objects are asteroids and comets.

Asteroids are small, rocky objects that orbit the sun. Many are in the asteroid belt between Mars and Jupiter.

Comets are balls that are mixtures of ice, rock, and dirt. They orbit the sun, too. Sometimes, when they get near the sun, some of their ice turns into gas. This gives comets tails that are millions of kilometers long.

What other objects can you see in the sky? In the night sky, we can see thousands of stars. They are all different sizes, ages, and colors. Some groups of stars seem to form shapes in the night sky. We call these groups of stars constellations. The Big Dipper and the Little Dipper are two well-known constellations. There are also many galaxies in the universe. Galaxies contain billions of stars. Our solar system is on the edge of the Milky Way Galaxy.

What other objects can we see in the sky?

asteroids

small, rocky objects orbiting the sun

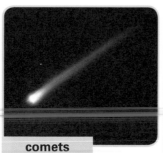

comets

bright objects with a long tail

constellations

groups of stars that form shapes

the Milky Way

the galaxy in which our solar system lies

Main Idea and Details

1 **What is the passage mainly about?**

   a. The solar system.   **b.** The constellations in the sky.

   c. Comets, asteroids, and stars.

2 **One well-known** _____ **is the Little Dipper.**

   a. constellation   **b.** comet   **c.** asteroid

3 **How many stars do galaxies contain?**

   a. Thousands.   **b.** Millions.   **c.** Billions.

4 **What does mixtures mean?**

   a. Combinations.   **b.** Recipes.   **c.** Amounts.

5 **According to the passage, which statement is true?**

   a. Some asteroids are bigger than the planets.

   b. Comets can have tails millions of kilometers long.

   c. There are only two constellations in the night sky.

6 **Complete the outline.**

Celestial Objects

Asteroids
- Are small, ᵃ_____ objects
- Orbit the sun
- Are many in the asteroid belt

Comets
- Are balls of ice, rock, and ᵇ_____
- Orbit the sun
- Get ᶜ_____ as they get near the sun
- Their tails can be millions of kilometers long.

Stars
- Can see thousands in the night sky
- Constellations = groups of stars that ᵈ_____ shapes
- Galaxies = billions of stars

Vocabulary Builder

Write the correct word and the meaning in Chinese.

1 ▸ an object in the sky

_____

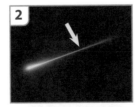
2 ▸ a long piece that extends from the back end or bottom of something

_____

3 ▸ the part of something that is farthest from its center

_____

4 ▸ a huge collection of billions of stars

_____

A Complete the sentences with the words below.

surface	instantly	weather	weathered
erosion	windstorms	collapse	broken

1 Weathering is the process by which large rocks are _____ down into small pieces.

2 Rushing water and strong winds can _____ rocks.

3 Erosion occurs when _____ rocks or soil are carried away to other places.

4 Weathering and _____ usually take thousands of years to change Earth's surface.

5 Earthquakes can _____ mountains and even change the routes that rivers and streams follow.

6 Volcanoes can also _____ change Earth's surface.

7 Hurricanes, tornadoes, and floods can change Earth's _____ quickly.

8 Tornadoes are powerful _____ that destroy most things in their paths.

B Complete the sentences with the words below.

Mercury	gases	well-known	separates
Galaxy	asteroids	solar system	mixtures

1 The _____ _____ is made up of the sun and all the objects that orbit it.

2 The inner planets are the four planets closest to the sun: _____, Venus, Earth, and Mars.

3 The outer planets are all huge and mostly made up of _____.

4 The asteroid belt _____ the inner planets from the outer planets.

5 _____ are small, rocky objects that orbit the sun.

6 Comets are balls that are _____ of ice, rock, and dirt.

7 The Big Dipper and the Little Dipper are two _____ constellations.

8 Our solar system is on the edge of the Milky Way _____.

C

Write the correct word and the meaning in Chinese.

1  ► the process of the carrying away of weathered rocks and soil

_____

2  ► the sudden shaking of Earth's surface

_____

3  ► melted rock from a volcano

_____

4  ► a small object that orbits a planet

_____

5 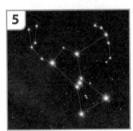 ► a group of stars that forms a shape

_____

6  ► an object in the sky that looks like a bright ball with a tail

_____

D

Match each word with the correct definition and write the meaning in Chinese.

1 weathering _____ ☐

2 weather _____ ☐

3 carry away _____ ☐

4 violent _____ ☐

5 route _____ ☐

6 moon _____ ☐

7 rocky _____ ☐

8 asteroid belt _____ ☐

9 celestial object _____ ☐

10 galaxy _____ ☐

a. an object in the sky

b. a way from one place to another

c. a small object that orbits a planet

d. a huge collection of billions of stars

e. covered with rocks or made of rocks

f. to move from one place to another

g. caused by destructive force; extreme

h. the belt of small objects between Mars and Jupiter

i. to change over a period of time because of rain, wind, etc.

j. the process of the breaking down of large rocks into small pieces

Key Words

- matter
- take up
- space
- mass
- property
- volume
- element
- substance
- hydrogen
- oxygen
- nitrogen
- helium
- compound
- atom
- particle
- molecule

Everything in the universe is made of matter. What is matter? Matter is anything that takes up space and has mass. All gases, liquids, and solids are made of matter.

Matter can be described by its properties. You can tell many kinds of matter apart by observing their color, size, shape, volume, and mass.

All matter is made of various elements. Elements are the basic substances that make up all the matter in the universe. There are more than 100 different elements. Some common elements are hydrogen, oxygen, nitrogen, and helium.

Elements can join together to form compounds. A compound is a substance that is formed by the chemical combination of two or more elements. For example, water is a compound made up of two elements: hydrogen and oxygen.

All elements are made of atoms. An atom is the smallest particle of matter. When two or more atoms join together, a molecule is created.

Common Elements and Their Symbols

Water Compound

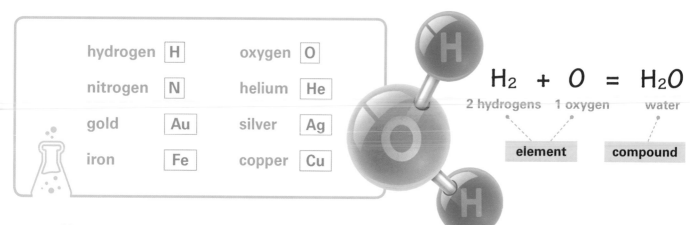

hydrogen	H	oxygen	O
nitrogen	N	helium	He
gold	Au	silver	Ag
iron	Fe	copper	Cu

$$H_2 + O = H_2O$$

2 hydrogens   1 oxygen   water

element   compound

Main Idea and Details

1 **What is the main idea of the passage?**
a. Everything is made up of matter.
b. There are more than 100 elements.
c. Elements can combine to form compounds.

2 **The basic substances that make up all matter are _____.**
a. molecules   b. elements   c. solids

3 **What is a compound?**
a. A solid, liquid, or a gas.
b. Anything that is made up of atoms.
c. The chemical joining of two or more elements.

4 **What does space mean?**
a. Temperature.   b. Time.   c. Room.

5 **Answer the questions.**
a. What is matter? _____
b. How many elements are there? _____
c. What is water? _____

6 **Complete the outline.**

Matter

What It Is
- Anything that takes up
  a _____ and has mass
- Includes all solids,
  liquids, and gases

Its Properties
- Can help describe matter
- Includes color, size, shape,
  b _____, and mass

Elements
- The c _____ substances
  that make up all matter
- There are more than 100.
- Can join together to form
  d _____

Vocabulary Builder

Write the correct word and the meaning in Chinese.

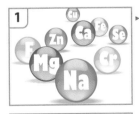 ▸ the basic substance that make up all the matter in the universe
_____

 ▸ any characteristics of matter that you can observe
_____

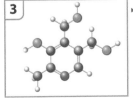 ▸ a substance that consists of two or more elements
_____

 ▸ the smallest particle of matter
_____

Changes in Matter

Matter often undergoes many changes. There are two kinds of changes: physical changes and chemical changes.

A physical change is a change that does not make a new substance. There are many ways matter can change physically. Matter can change states. For example, you can find water in its solid state, liquid state, or gas state. It looks different in each state, but it is still the same kind of matter. Making a solution is another example of a physical change. If you pour salt into water and stir it, it will dissolve. You cannot see the salt anymore, but the salt is still there.

Matter can also undergo chemical changes. Chemical changes involve the forming of a new compound. For instance, hydrogen and oxygen are usually two separate gases. However, if you combine two hydrogen atoms with one oxygen atom, you get water. This is a chemical change.

Key Words

- undergo
- physical change
- chemical change
- physically
- state
- solution
- pour
- stir
- dissolve
- involve
- combine

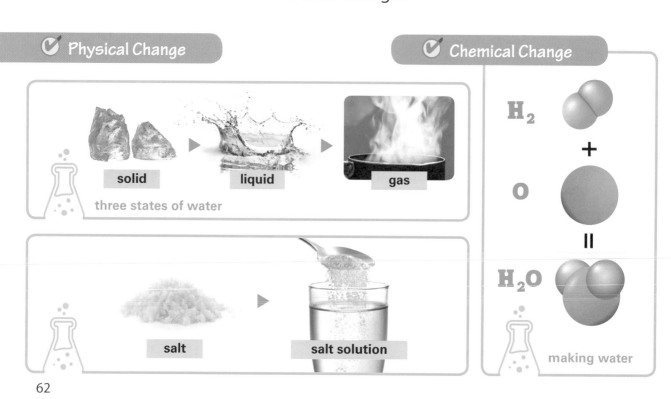

Physical Change

solid → liquid → gas

three states of water

salt → salt solution

Chemical Change

H_2 + O = H_2O

making water

Main Idea and Details

1 **What is the main idea of the passage?**

    a. Water has solid, liquid, and gas states.

    b. Matter can change physically or chemically.

    c. It is possible to change the physical states of matter.

2 **Salt will _____ when it is stirred in water.**

    a. dissolve   **b.** separate   **c.** undergo

3 **What is water made of?**

    a. Two oxygen atoms and one hydrogen atom.

    b. One oxygen atom and two hydrogen atoms.

    c. One oxygen atom and one hydrogen atom.

4 **What does substance mean?**

    a. Atom.   **b.** Solution.   **c.** Matter.

5 **Complete the sentences.**

    a. Matter can change _____ from a solid to a liquid to a gas.

    b. There are both _____ changes and chemical changes.

    c. A new compound forms in a _____ change.

6 **Complete the outline.**

Changes in Matter

Physical Change
- Does not make a new substance
- Can change ^{a}_____ from solid to liquid to gas
- Can make a ^{b}_____

Chemical Change
- Forms a new ^{c}_____
- Two hydrogen atoms + one oxygen atom = ^{d}_____

Vocabulary Builder

Write the correct word and the meaning in Chinese.

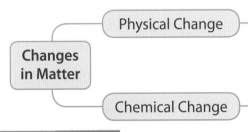 ► a change that forms a new compound

_____

 ► to melt; to make a solution

_____

 ► a change that does not make a new substance

_____

 ► to mix something by moving it around with a spoon or a stick

_____

Taking Care of Our Bodies

Key Words

- **get sick**
- **catch a cold**
- **the flu**
- **disease**
- **illness**
- **germ**
- **virus**
- **bacterium**
  (*pl.* **bacteria**)
- **shot**
- **spread**
- **good hygiene**
- **balanced diet**
- **junk food**

We sometimes get sick. We may catch a cold, the flu, or some other disease. These illnesses are caused by germs such as viruses and bacteria.

When we get sick, we usually go to the doctor. The doctor may give us a shot or some medicine. After a few days, we typically get better.

However, many illnesses, like colds and the flu, can spread from one person to another. To stay healthy and strong, we need to practice healthy habits.

First, we need to practice good hygiene. We should wash our hands often. We should always wash our hands after using the bathroom and before eating.

Also, we need to exercise. Exercise keeps our bodies healthy and strong. It also helps our bodies fight disease.

Eating a balanced diet is also very important. Healthy foods give our bodies energy to work. Unhealthy foods like junk food can make you get sick more frequently.

Taking Care of Our Bodies

We should wash our hands often.

We need to exercise.

We need to eat a balanced diet.

We should avoid unhealthy foods.

Main Idea and Details

1 **What is the passage mainly about?**

   a. How a person can stay healthy.

   b. What kind of food a person should eat.

   c. Which sicknesses a person can get.

2 **A person should exercise to become _____ and strong.**

   a. clean   **b.** balanced   **c.** healthy

3 **What is washing one's hands an example of?**

   a. A balanced diet.   **b.** Exercise.   **c.** Good hygiene.

4 **What does junk mean?**

   a. Garbage.   **b.** Candy.   **c.** Unbalanced.

5 **According to the passage, which statement is true?**

   a. People can get the flu from exercising.

   b. Viruses and bacteria can make people sick.

   c. It is okay to eat a lot of junk food.

6 **Complete the outline.**

Healthy Habits

Good Hygiene
- Is important to stay healthy
- Wash your hands before eating and after using the
  ᵃ _____

Exercise
- Keeps bodies healthy and strong
- Helps bodies ᵇ_____ diseases

Balanced Diets
- Give bodies ᶜ_____ to work
- Unhealthy foods make people ᵈ_____.

Vocabulary Builder

Write the correct word and the meaning in Chinese.

 **1** ▸ a common disease that is like a bad cold

_____

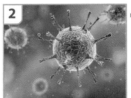 **2** ▸ a simple living thing that is smaller than bacteria and that can enter your body and make you sick

_____

 **3** ▸ the act of putting medicine into your body by using a needle

_____

 **4** ▸ food that tastes good but is high in calories having little nutritional value

_____

24

Key Words

- nutrient
- carbohydrate
- protein
- fat
- vitamin
- mineral
- sugar
- starch
- cell
- repair
- dairy product
- muscle
- nervous system
- remove
- waste

Your body's systems need nutrients to function properly. Nutrients are materials in food that your body uses to grow and to stay healthy.

There are six kinds of nutrients. They are carbohydrates, proteins, fats, vitamins, minerals, and water. Each nutrient helps the body in a different way.

Carbohydrates are main source of energy for your body. There are two kinds of carbohydrates: sugars and starches. Foods with starches include rice, potatoes, and bread. Fruits such as apples and oranges are made of sugars.

Proteins are part of every living cell. The body needs many proteins to grow and to repair body cells. Meat, fish, milk, eggs, and dairy products contain proteins.

Fats help your body use other nutrients and store energy. But they are needed only in small amounts. Fats are found in meats, butter, milk, and oils.

Vitamins protect you from illnesses. Minerals help your blood, muscles, and nervous system.

Water helps your body remove wastes. It also keeps your body temperature normal. You could not live for even a week without water.

The Six Nutrients and Food

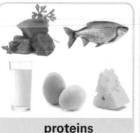

| carbohydrates | proteins | fats | vitamins and minerals | water |

Main Idea and Details

1 **What is the main idea of the passage?**

a. People will die without any water.

b. Everyone needs carbohydrates and proteins.

c. The body needs several important nutrients.

2 **What are sugars and starches?**

a. Fats.   b. Carbohydrates.   c. Proteins.

3 **What helps your body remove wastes?**

a. Vitamin.   b. Mineral.   c. Water.

4 **What does repair mean?**

a. Make.   b. Fix.   c. Protect.

5 **Complete the sentences.**

a. Rice, potatoes, and bread all have _____.

b. The body needs _____ to grow and to repair cells.

c. The body needs _____ to be safe from illnesses.

6 **Complete the outline.**

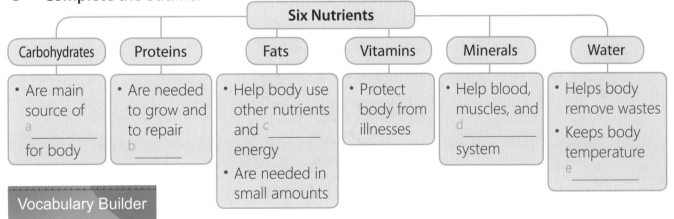

Six Nutrients

Carbohydrates	Proteins	Fats	Vitamins	Minerals	Water
• Are main source of a_____ for body	• Are needed to grow and to repair b_____	• Help body use other nutrients and c_____ energy • Are needed in small amounts	• Protect body from illnesses	• Help blood, muscles, and d_____ system	• Helps body remove wastes • Keeps body temperature e_____

Vocabulary Builder

Write the correct word and the meaning in Chinese.

 ▸ the main source of energy for the body

_____

 ▸ It protects you from illnesses.

_____

 ▸ It helps the body grow and repair cells.

_____

 ▸ milk and butter and cheese

_____

Vocabulary **Review 6**

A Complete the sentences with the words below.

> substance described combine involve
> molecule space solution elements

1 Matter is anything that takes up _____ and has mass.

2 Matter can be _____ by its properties.

3 A compound is a substance that is formed by the chemical combination of two or more _____.

4 When two or more atoms join together, a _____ is created.

5 A physical change is a change that does not make a new _____.

6 Making a _____ is another example of a physical change.

7 Chemical changes _____ the forming of a new compound.

8 If you _____ two hydrogen atoms with one oxygen atom, you get water.

B Complete the sentences with the words below.

> cold carbohydrates hygiene function
> germs junk food normal repair

1 We may catch a _____, the flu, or some other disease.

2 These illnesses are caused by _____ such as viruses and bacteria.

3 To stay healthy and strong, we need to practice good _____.

4 Unhealthy foods like _____ _____ can make you get sick more frequently.

5 Your body's systems need nutrients to _____ properly.

6 _____ are main source of energy for your body.

7 The body needs many proteins to grow and to _____ body cells.

8 Water keeps your body temperature _____.

C Write the correct word and the meaning in Chinese.

 ► physical matter or material

_____

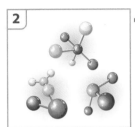 ► the smallest part of an element or compound that is composed of one or more atoms

_____

 ► a change that forms a new compound

_____

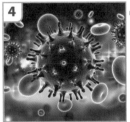 ► a simple living thing that is smaller than bacteria and that can enter your body and make you sick

_____

 ► the act of putting medicine into your body by using a needle

_____

 ► It helps the body use other nutrients and store energy.

_____

D Match each word with the correct definition and write the meaning in Chinese.

1 take up   _____ ☐

2 property   _____ ☐

3 dissolve   _____ ☐

4 involve   _____ ☐

5 combine   _____ ☐

6 disease   _____ ☐

7 hygiene   _____ ☐

8 carbohydrate   _____ ☐

9 protein   _____ ☐

10 remove   _____ ☐

a. to join

b. to occupy; to fill

c. to melt; to make a solution

d. the main source of energy for the body

e. It helps the body grow and repair cells.

f. to include or affect someone or something

g. any characteristics of matter that you can observe

h. the practice of keeping yourself and your surroundings clean

i. to take something away from the place where it is

j. an illness which is caused by bacteria or an infection

Wrap-Up Test **2**

A Write the correct word for each sentence.

> carried away   life cycle   larva   process   fats
> gas giants   instinctive   match   thousands   inner

1   Some animals undergo big _____ _____ changes called metamorphosis.

2   In the second stage, a tiny caterpillar, or _____, hatches from the egg.

3   Migration and hibernation are both _____ behaviors.

4   Many animals have body colors or shapes that _____ their surroundings.

5   Weathering is the _____ by which large rocks are broken down into small pieces.

6   Erosion occurs when weathered rocks or soil are _____ _____ to other places.

7   Weathering and erosion usually take _____ of years to change Earth's surface.

8   The asteroid belt separates the _____ planets from the outer planets.

9   The outer planets are often called _____ _____.

10   _____ help your body use other nutrients and store energy.

B Write the meanings of the words in Chinese.

1	hatch		16	weathering
2	metamorphosis		17	weather
3	caterpillar		18	carry away
4	cocoon		19	violent
5	camouflage		20	route
6	fertilized egg		21	moon
7	spin thread		22	asteroid belt
8	instinct		23	celestial object
9	behavior		24	galaxy
10	hibernate		25	take up
11	adaptation		26	property
12	mimicry		27	dissolve
13	erosion		28	involve
14	erupt		29	hygiene
15	constellation		30	element

3

- **Mathematics**
- **Language**
- **Visual Arts**
- **Music**

Fractions

Key Words

- whole number
- equal part
- fraction
- numerator
- denominator
- represent
- in the whole
- be counted
- mixed number
- equivalent fraction
- value
- unit fraction

Sometimes, we divide whole numbers into equal parts. We can express these numbers as fractions. For example, if something is divided into two equal parts, we can describe one part as $\frac{1}{2}$. $\frac{1}{2}$ is written in words as one half. If something is divided into three equal parts, each part is $\frac{1}{3}$. $\frac{1}{3}$ is written in words as one third.

A fraction has a top number and a bottom number. The top number is the numerator. And the bottom number is the denominator. The denominator represents how many equal parts there are in the whole. The numerator represents how many equal parts are being counted.

A mixed number is a combination of a whole number and a fraction. $1\frac{1}{2}$, $2\frac{3}{4}$, and $3\frac{4}{5}$ are mixed numbers.

There are also equivalent fractions. These fractions have equal values but use different numbers. $\frac{1}{2}$ and $\frac{2}{4}$ are equivalent fractions. So are $\frac{2}{3}$ and $\frac{6}{9}$.

A fraction that has a numerator of 1, such as $\frac{1}{2}$ and $\frac{1}{3}$, is called a unit fraction.

✓ A fraction is a part of something.

				numerator
$\frac{1}{2}$	$\frac{1}{3}$	$\frac{1}{4}$	$\frac{2}{5}$	denominator

mixed number	**equivalent fraction**	**unit fraction**
$1\frac{1}{2}$, $2\frac{3}{4}$, $3\frac{4}{5}$	$\frac{1}{2}=\frac{2}{4}$, $\frac{2}{3}=\frac{6}{9}$	$\frac{1}{2}$, $\frac{1}{3}$

Main Idea and Details

1   What is the main idea of the passage?
   a. There are equivalent fractions and unit fractions.
   b. We can write some numbers as fractions.
   c. A fraction has a numerator and a denominator.

2   A whole number and a fraction together make _____.
   a. a mixed number   **b.** a unit fraction   **c.** an equivalent fraction

3   What is a denominator?
   a. The top number of a fraction.   **b.** The bottom number of a fraction.
   c. A whole number and a fraction.

4   What does represents mean?
   a. Changes.   **b.** Means.   **c.** Shows.

5   Complete the sentences.
   a. $\frac{1}{3}$ represents something divided into _____ equal parts.
   b. $2\frac{3}{4}$ is a _____ number.   **c.** $\frac{1}{2}$ and $\frac{3}{6}$ are _____ fractions.

6   Complete the outline.

Fractions

What They Are	Mixed Numbers	Equivalent Fractions	Unit Fractions
• Are numbers divided into ^a_____ parts • Numerator = top number • Denominator = ^b_____ number	• Are ^c_____ of whole numbers and fractions, such as $1\frac{1}{2}$ and $2\frac{3}{4}$	• Are fractions with equal ^d_____ but use different numbers, such as $\frac{1}{2}$ and $\frac{2}{4}$	• Are fractions that have a ^e_____ of 1, such as $\frac{1}{2}$ and $\frac{1}{3}$

Vocabulary Builder

Write the correct word and the meaning in Chinese.

 ▸ the top number of a fraction
   _____

▸ the bottom number of a fraction
   _____

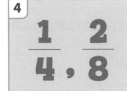 ▸ a combination of a whole number and a fraction
   _____

▸ fractions that have equal values but use different numbers
   _____

Key Words

- shaded
- solution
- compare
- greater
- equivalent
- piece
- slice

1 Here is a circle. Write how many equal parts there are. And write the fraction that names the shaded part.

Solution: There are six equal parts. $\frac{3}{6}$ (three sixths) of the whole is shaded.

2 Compare $\frac{1}{4}$ and $\frac{2}{4}$. Which one is greater?

Solution: $\frac{2}{4}$ is greater than $\frac{1}{4}$.

When two fractions have the same denominator, the one with the greater numerator is the greater fraction.

3 Compare $\frac{1}{4}$ and $\frac{1}{8}$. Which one is greater?

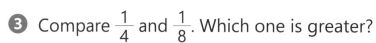

Solution: $\frac{1}{4}$ is greater than $\frac{1}{8}$.

When you compare or add two fractions with different denominators, you need to make the denominator the same. $\frac{1}{4}$ and $\frac{2}{8}$ are equivalent fractions. $\frac{1}{4} = \frac{2}{8}$. So, $\frac{2}{8} > \frac{1}{8}$.

4 Mom cuts an apple into different pieces. She gives $\frac{1}{4}$ of the apple to Cindy. And she gives $\frac{1}{2}$ of the apple to Jane. Who has the bigger piece of the apple?

Solution: $\frac{1}{2}$ is greater than $\frac{1}{4}$. ($\frac{1}{2} = \frac{2}{4}$. So, $\frac{2}{4} > \frac{1}{4}$)

So, Jane has the bigger piece of the apple.

5 David orders a pizza and slices it into 12 slices. David takes $\frac{1}{3}$ of the pizza. And Steve takes $\frac{1}{4}$ of the pizza. How much of the pizza do they take together?

Solution: $\frac{1}{3} = \frac{4}{12}$. And $\frac{1}{4} = \frac{3}{12}$. So, $\frac{4}{12} + \frac{3}{12} = \frac{7}{12}$.

Together, they take $\frac{7}{12}$ of the pizza.

Main Idea and Details

1   **What is the passage mainly about?**
  a. Determining the values of fractions.
  b. Adding fractions together.
  c. Subtracting fractions from one another.

2 $\frac{1}{4}$ is _____ $\frac{1}{8}$.
  a. greater than   **b.** less than   **c.** equal to

3   **What should you do when you add two fractions with different denominators?**
  a. Add the lowest number first.
  b. Multiply the fractions.
  c. Make the denominators the same.

4   **What does pieces mean?**
  a. Styles.   **b.** Halves.   **c.** Slices.

5   **According to the passage, which statement is true?**
  a. $\frac{1}{4}$ is greater than $\frac{1}{2}$.   **b.** $\frac{1}{2}$ is greater than $\frac{1}{4}$.   **c.** $\frac{1}{4}$ is greater than $\frac{1}{3}$.

6   **Answer the questions.**
  a. When two fractions have the same denominator, which one is greater?

  _____

  b. What do you call the fractions $\frac{1}{4}$ and $\frac{2}{8}$? _____

  c. Write how many equal parts there are.

     _____

Vocabulary Builder

Write the correct word and the meaning in Chinese.

1	▸ dark; colored darker than the surroundings

_____

2	▸ to examine or judge two or more things

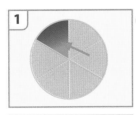

_____

3	▸ the answer to a problem in mathematics

$\frac{1}{4}$ is greater than $\frac{1}{8}$.

_____

4	▸ to cut; to divide into pieces; a piece

_____

Understanding Decimals

Key Words

- decimal
- period
- decimal point
- digit
- tenths place
- hundredths place
- thousandths place
- be equivalent to
- ones place

You can write the fraction $\frac{1}{10}$ as the decimal 0.1. The period to the left of the 1 is called a decimal point.

A decimal is a number with one or more digits to the right of the decimal point. The first place to the right of the decimal point is the tenths place. The second place to the right of the decimal point is the hundredths place. The fraction $\frac{1}{100}$ can also be written as the decimal 0.01. The third place to the right of the decimal point is the thousandths place. The fraction $\frac{1}{1000}$ can also be written as the decimal 0.001. You can say $\frac{1}{1000}$ is equivalent to 0.001.

Place	Ones		Tenths	Hundredths	Thousandths
	0	.	1		
Value	0	.	0	1	
	0	.	0	0	1

You can write the mixed number $1\frac{2}{10}$ as the decimal 1.2. The mixed number $2\frac{15}{100}$ is 2.15 as a decimal.

Place	Ones		Tenths	Hundredths
Value	1	.	2	
	2	.	1	5

As you read above, you can change a decimal to an equivalent fraction and a fraction to an equivalent decimal. Let's practice changing decimals to equivalent fractions. And, for each fraction, write the equivalent decimal.

1. $0.4 = (\frac{4}{10})$

2. $\frac{4}{100} = (0.04)$

3. $0.78 = (\frac{78}{100})$

4. $1\frac{30}{100} = (1.30)$

Main Idea and Details

1 **What is the passage mainly about?**

   a. How to write decimals.   **b.** How to make fractions.

   c. How to subtract decimals from fractions.

2 **We can write the fraction $\frac{1}{100}$ as _____ .**

   a. 0.1   **b.** 0.01   **c.** 0.001

3 **What is the third place to the right of the decimal point?**

   a. The tenths place.   **b.** The hundredths place.   **c.** The thousandths place.

4 **What does digits mean?**

   a. Numbers.   **b.** Places.   **c.** Fractions.

5 **Answer the questions.**

   a. What is the period that starts a decimal called? _____

   b. How can you write 0.001 as a fraction? _____

   c. What is the second place to the right of the decimal point? _____

6 **Complete the outline.**

Decimals

What They Are

- Are numbers with one or more digits to the right of the decimal point
- a_____ _____ = the first place to the right of the decimal point
- Hundredths place = the second place to the right of the decimal point
- Thousandths place = the b_____ _____ to the right of the decimal point

Decimals and Fractions

- Can write decimals as c_____
- $0.1 = \frac{1}{10}$
- $0.01 = $ d_____
- $0.001 = \frac{1}{1000}$

Vocabulary Builder

Write the correct word and the meaning in Chinese.

1

0.25
▸ the period that starts a decimal
_____

2
0 1 2 3 4
5 6 7 8 9
▸ any of the numbers from 0 to 9
_____

3
3.45
▸ the first place to the right of the decimal point
_____

4

6.15
▸ the place just to the left of the decimal point
_____

Reading and Writing Fractions and Decimals

Key Words

- confusing
- cardinal number
- ordinal number
- fourth
- ninth
- fifteenth
- individually
- point
- zero

It can sometimes look confusing to read or write a fraction or decimal. But it is actually really easy.

For fractions, the easiest way is to read the numerator as a cardinal number and the denominator as an ordinal number. So, $\frac{1}{4}$ = one fourth, $\frac{4}{9}$ = four ninths, and $\frac{7}{15}$ = seven fifteenths.

But there are other ways to read fractions, too. You could say the fraction $\frac{3}{4}$ is three fourths, three out of four, or three divided by four. So the fraction $\frac{2}{3}$ is two thirds, two out of three, or two divided by three.

Reading decimals is much easier. Just say each number individually. For example, 2.1 is two point one. 3.14 is three point one four. If there is a zero in front of the decimal point, you must say that, too. So 0.1 is zero point one.

You can also read some decimals as fractions. For instance, 0.5 is zero point five or one half. 0.33 is zero point three three or one third.

✓ Reading and Writing Fractions

$\dfrac{1}{4}$
= one fourth
= one out of four
= one divided by four

$\dfrac{4}{9}$
= four ninths
= four out of nine
= four divided by nine

$\frac{2}{3}$ = ?

1.8 = ?

✓ Reading and Writing Decimals

2.1 = two point one   **0.1** = zero point one

3.14 = three point one four   **0.5** = zero point five = one half

1 **What is the main idea of the passage?**

   a. It is easy to read and write fractions and decimals.

   b. It is possible to write a fraction as a decimal.

   c. It is all right to convert decimals into fractions.

2 **We can read $\frac{1}{4}$ as _____.**

   a. one half   **b.** one third   **c.** one fourth

3 **How do you read decimals?**

   a. You read the numbers like fractions.   **b.** You read the numbers from right to left.

   c. You read each number individually.

4 **What does confusing mean?**

   a. Exciting.   **b.** Puzzling.   **c.** Interesting.

5 **Complete the sentences.**

   a. We can write two thirds as _____.

   b. We can read the fraction $\frac{3}{4}$ as three out of _____.

   c. We can read the decimal 3.14 as three _____ one four.

6 **Complete the outline.**

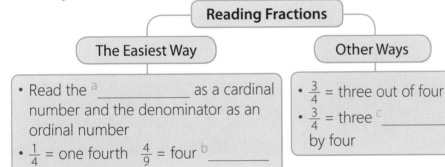

Reading Fractions

The Easiest Way
- Read the ᵃ_____ as a cardinal number and the denominator as an ordinal number
- $\frac{1}{4}$ = one fourth $\frac{4}{9}$ = four ᵇ_____

Other Ways
- $\frac{3}{4}$ = three out of four
- $\frac{3}{4}$ = three ᶜ_____ by four

Reading Decimals
- Say each number individually
- 3.14 = three point one four
- 0.1 = ᵈ_____ point one

Write the correct word and the meaning in Chinese.

1

0

▸ the number 0

_____

2

1, 2, 3, 4, 5...

▸ a number, such as 1 and 2, that shows the quantity of something

_____

3

1st, 2nd, 3rd, 4th, 5th...

▸ a number, such as first and second, that shows the order of something

_____

4

2.1

▸ separately

_____

Review 7

A

Complete the sentences with the words below.

divided	whole	equal parts	compare
equal	slices	combination	greater

1   Sometimes, we divide whole numbers into _____ _____.

2   If something is _____ into three equal parts, each part is $\frac{1}{3}$.

3   A mixed number is a _____ of a whole number and a fraction.

4   Equivalent fractions have _____ values but use different numbers.

5   The denominator represents how many equal parts there are in the _____.

6   When two fractions have the same denominator, the one with the _____ numerator is the greater fraction.

7   _____ $\frac{1}{4}$ and $\frac{1}{8}$. Which one is greater?

8   David orders a pizza and slices it into 12 _____.

B

Complete the sentences with the words below.

cardinal	decimal point	digits	hundredths
equivalent	decimal	fractions	individually

1   You can write the fraction $\frac{1}{10}$ as the _____ 0.1.

2   A decimal is a number with one or more _____ to the right of the decimal point.

3   The second place to the right of the decimal point is the _____ place.

4   You can say $\frac{1}{1000}$ is _____ to 0.001.

5   For fractions, the easiest way is to read the numerator as a _____ number and the denominator as an ordinal number.

6   Reading decimals is much easier. Just say each number _____.

7   If there is a zero in front of the _____ _____, you must say that, too.

8   You can also read some decimals as _____.

C
Write the correct word and the meaning in Chinese.

1

$$\frac{5}{6}$$

▸ the top number of a fraction

_____

2

$1\frac{2}{3}, 5\frac{4}{9}$

▸ a combination of a whole number and a fraction

_____

3

0.25

▸ the first place to the right of the decimal point

_____

4

1st, 2nd, 3rd, 4th, 5th...

▸ a number, such as first and second, that shows the order of something

_____

5

1, 2, 3, 4, 5...

▸ a number, such as 1 and 2, that shows the quantity of something

_____

6

0 1 2 3 4 5 6 7 8 9

▸ any of the numbers from 0 to 9

_____

D
Match each word with the correct definition and write the meaning in Chinese.

1 numerator _____ ☐

2 unit fraction _____ ☐

3 shaded _____ ☐

4 compare _____ ☐

5 equivalent _____ ☐

6 slice _____ ☐

7 tenths place _____ ☐

8 be equivalent to _____ ☐

9 confusing _____ ☐

10 individually _____ ☐

a. separately

b. to be equal to

c. the top number of a fraction

d. to cut; to divide into pieces; a piece

e. a fraction that has a numerator of 1

f. to examine or judge two or more things

g. dark; colored darker than the surroundings

h. the first place to the right of the decimal point

i. difficult to understand because something is unclear

j. having the same value or naming the same amount

81

Stories and Myths
Norse Mythology

Key Words

- Norse
- mythology (= myth)
- Scandinavian
- Scandinavia
- Viking
- Norseman
- legend
- chief
- raven
- mighty
- thunderbolt
- trickster
- battle
- troll
- hold up

Norse mythology tells stories from Scandinavian countries in Northwest Europe. Today, Scandinavia includes Norway, Sweden, Finland, and Denmark.

A long time ago, many Vikings lived in Scandinavia. The Vikings were also called Norsemen. Like the ancient Greeks and Romans, the Vikings had their own myths and legends. Today, we call these stories Norse mythology.

In Norse mythology, there were many gods and goddesses. Odin was the chief god. He always had two ravens, Thought and Memory. Thor, son of Odin, was the god of thunder. When he swung his mighty hammer, thunderbolts struck, and rain fell onto the earth. Loki was the trickster god. Odin's wife Frigg and Thor's wife Freya were two important goddesses. And there were many other gods and goddesses, too.

The Norse gods all lived in a land called Asgard. They constantly battled monsters such as frost giants and trolls. The Vikings believed that a giant "world tree" called Yggdrasil held up the universe. One day, the tree would fall and bring down the world, causing a great battle between the gods and giants. Eventually, the giants would win this battle at Ragnarök and the world would be destroyed. This was the end of the world in Norse mythology.

giant

Norse Gods and Goddesses

Odin's two ravens, Thought and Memory

Odin

Thor

Loki

Frigg

Freya

Main Idea and Details

1 **What is the passage mainly about?**

  a. Gods and other creatures in Norse mythology.

  b. The most powerful gods in Norse mythology.

  c. The land of Asgard and the creatures in it.

2 _____ **was the battle where the gods would lose.**

  a. Asgard   **b.** Ragnarök   **c.** Scandinavia

3 **What was Yggdrasil?**

  a. The land of the gods in Norse mythology.

  b. The world tree that held up the universe.

  c. A battle between the gods and giants.

4 **What does mighty mean?**

  a. Heavy.   **b.** Magical.   **c.** Powerful.

5 **According to the passage, which statement is true?**

  a. Odin and Freya were married.

  b. Thor was a son of Odin and the god of thunder.

  c. Loki and Thor were brothers.

6 **Complete the outline.**

Norse Mythology

Gods and Goddesses

- Odin = the ᵃ_____ god
- Thor = the god of ᵇ_____
- Loki = the trickster god
- Frigg = Odin's wife
- Freya = Thor's wife

Other Aspects

- ᶜ_____ = the land where the gods lived
- Monsters = frost giants and trolls
- Yggdrasil = the ᵈ_____ _____
- Ragnarök = the great battle at the end of the world

Vocabulary Builder

Write the correct word and the meaning in Chinese.

1  ▸ a Scandinavian pirate from the 8th to 10th centuries

_____

2  ▸ relating to ancient Scandinavia

_____

3  ▸ a flash of lightning that hits something

_____

4  ▸ someone who uses dishonest methods to get what they want

_____

Stories and Myths
Loki the Trickster

Loki was the trickster in Norse mythology. He was the father of Fenrir, the great wolf, and of Hel, the goddess of the dead. He often caused many problems for the gods, especially Thor. But he could help them, too.

Key Words

- trickster
- frost
- hammer
- refuse
- get married
- play a trick on
- dress up
- servant
- in disguise
- veil
- ceremony

One day, the frost giant Thrym stole Thor's great hammer. Thrym said he would return the hammer if he could marry Thor's wife Freya. Freya refused, so Loki had an idea. He told Thor to agree to Thrym's suggestion. But Freya would not really get married. Instead, they would play a trick on the giant.

Loki dressed up as Freya's servant. And Thor dressed up as Freya. Together, they traveled to the giants' land. There, Loki told the giants that Freya was ready to marry Thrym. But it was really Thor in disguise. At the wedding party, Thor ate and drank very much. Loki explained, "Freya is excited to get married. So she is hungry." Thrym wanted to kiss Freya. He lifted the veil and saw Thor's red eyes. Loki explained, "Freya is so excited that she hasn't slept for eight days. So her eyes are red."

During the ceremony, Thrym gave "Freya" the hammer. Thor quickly grabbed it and killed all of the giants.

Main Idea and Details

1   **What is the passage mainly about?**

a. How Thor got his hammer back from the giants.

b. The marriage of Freya and Thrym.

c. Why no one could ever trust Loki.

2   **The giant who stole Thor's hammer was called _____.**

a. Freya   b. Loki   c. Thrym

3   **What did Thrym see when he lifted the veil?**

a. He saw Thor's beard.   b. He saw Thor's red eyes.

c. He saw Thor's mouth.

4   **What does suggestion mean?**

a. Proposal.   b. Demand.   c. Purpose.

5   **Answer the questions.**

a. Who was Loki the father of? _____

b. What did Thrym want in return for Thor's hammer? _____

c. What did Thor do when he got his hammer back? _____

6   **Complete the outline.**

Loki the Trickster

Thor's Hammer	Loki's Idea	The End Result
• Thrym steals Thor's ^a_____. • Will give the hammer back if he can ^b_____ Freya • Freya refuses.	• They will play a ^c_____ on the giants. • Thor dresses up as Freya. • They go to the frost giants' land and pretend to get married.	• Giants don't realize that Thor is ^d_____ _____ as Freya. • Thor gets his hammer back. • Thor kills all of the giants.

Vocabulary Builder

Write the correct word and the meaning in Chinese.

 **1** ▸ to reject; to turn down

_____

 **2** ▸ a person working in the service of another

_____

 **3** ▸ to put on a disguise or outfit

_____

 **4** ▸ a thin white layer of ice that forms on things outside when the weather is very cold

_____

Key Words

- declarative
- interrogative
- imperative
- exclamatory
- statement
- period
- question mark
- command
- order
- direction
- exclamation
- exclamation point

When we speak, we use four different kinds of sentences. They are declarative, interrogative, imperative, and exclamatory sentences.

A declarative sentence makes a statement about something. So, it is also called a statement. We use a period to end a declarative sentence:

▸ I like English.
▸ Mr. Johnson lives in the city.
▸ There are three pencils in the pencil case.

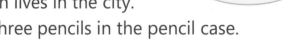

I like English.

We use interrogative sentences to ask questions. An interrogative sentence is also called a question. These sentences end with a question mark:

▸ What time is it?
▸ Where are you going?
▸ What will I be when I grow up?

What time is it?

Where are you going?

An imperative sentence or a command gives orders or directions. In an imperative sentence, the subject of the sentence is "you." But you do not say "you." These sentences end with a period or an exclamation point:

▸ Open the door.
▸ Be quiet!
▸ Go home right now.

Be quiet!

We use exclamatory sentences or exclamations when we are surprised or excited about something. These sentences end with an exclamation point:

▸ That's amazing!
▸ I can't believe it!
▸ Ouch!

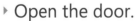

Ouch!

Main Idea and Details

1   What is the main idea of the passage?

    a. There are several types of sentences.

    b. Declarative sentences are the most common.

    c. Interrogative sentences need a question mark.

2   You should use _____ after an exclamatory sentence.

    a. a question mark   **b.** a period   **c.** an exclamation point

3   What is an imperative sentence?

    a. A question.   **b.** A command.   **c.** An exclamation.

4   What does directions mean?

    a. Questions.   **b.** Instructions.   **c.** Sentences.

5   Complete the sentences.

    a. A _____ sentence is a statement about something.

    b. _____ sentences always end with question marks.

    c. Exclamatory sentences show _____ or excitement.

6   Complete the outline.

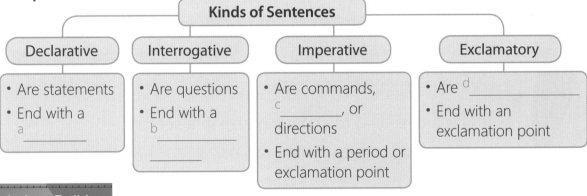

Kinds of Sentences

Declarative	Interrogative	Imperative	Exclamatory
• Are statements • End with a a _____	• Are questions • End with a b _____	• Are commands, c _____, or directions • End with a period or exclamation point	• Are d _____ • End with an exclamation point

Vocabulary Builder

Write the correct word and the meaning in Chinese.

1 What is it? ▸ a sentence type that asks questions

_____

2 I have a dog. ▸ a sentence type that states something

_____

3 How beautiful! ▸ a sentence type that shows surprise or excitement

_____

4 Stop it! ▸ a sentence type that gives orders or directions

_____

There are many kinds of punctuation marks in English. We use them in different situations.

Key Words

- punctuation mark
- end with
- comma
- pause
- colon
- list
- explanation
- dash
- quotes
- semicolon
- hyphen
- slash

We always use a punctuation mark at the end of a sentence. Most sentences end with a period (.). However, if you are asking a question, use a question mark (?) at the end. If you are making an exclamation, use an exclamation point (!) at the end.

But we also use punctuation marks in the middle of a sentence. One common punctuation mark is a comma (,). A comma is like a pause in the middle of a sentence. The following sentences need commas:

> ‣ I like apples, oranges, and bananas.
> ‣ Eric is a student, but John is a teacher.

Use a colon (:) to list things or add explanations:

> ‣ You can use a colon in several ways: to make lists or to give explanations.

Use a dash (—) to show a pause in a sentence:

> ‣ Jay—my brother—is going to do his homework right now.

And use quotes (" ") to show that a person is speaking:

> ‣ He said, "Please open the door."

There are also other punctuation marks, such as a semicolon (;), hyphen (-), and slash (/).

✓ Punctuation Marks

.	?	!	,	:	;	" "	—	-	/
period	question mark	exclamation point	comma	colon	semicolon	quotes	dash	hyphen	slash

Main Idea and Details

1 **What is the passage mainly about?**

a. The difference between periods and commas.

b. How to use quotes and commas.

c. Punctuation marks that can be used in different situations.

2 **You can use _____ to show that a person is speaking.**

a. quotes   **b.** slash   **c.** comma

3 **What does a colon look like?**

a. !   **b.** :   **c.** ;

4 **What does pause mean?**

a. Break.   **b.** End.   **c.** Topic.

5 **According to the passage, which statement is true?**

a. A comma is a pause in the middle of a sentence.

b. A hyphen is used for exclamations.

c. A dash can connect two sentences.

6 **Complete the outline.**

Punctuation Marks

At the Ends of Sentences

- ᵃ _____ (.)
  = Most sentences end with it.
- Question mark (?)
  = used for questions
- Exclamation point (!)
  = used for exclamations

Pauses

- Comma (,)
  = a ᵇ _____ in the middle of a sentence
- ᶜ _____ (—)
  = a pause in a sentence

Other Punctuation

- Colon (:) = to list things or add explanations
- Quotes (" ") = to show that a person is speaking
- ᵈ _____ (;), hyphen (-), and slash (/)

Vocabulary Builder

Write the correct word and the meaning in Chinese.

1  ▸ a mark such as a comma, colon, and question mark

_____

2 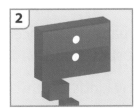 ▸ a punctuation mark used to list things or add explanations

_____

3  ▸ a punctuation mark used to show that a person is speaking

_____

4  ▸ a punctuation mark used for questions

_____

Vocabulary **Review 8**

A Complete the sentences with the words below.

chief	dressed up	Asgard	held up
trickster	Scandinavian	grabbed	hammer

1　Norse mythology tells stories from _____ countries in Northwest Europe.

2　Odin was the _____ god. He always had two ravens, Thought and Memory.

3　The Norse gods all lived in a land called _____.

4　The Vikings believed that a giant "world tree" called Yggdrasil _____ _____ the universe.

5　Loki was the _____ in Norse mythology.

6　One day, the frost giant Thrym stole Thor's great _____.

7　Loki dressed up as Freya's servant. And Thor _____ _____ as Freya.

8　Thor quickly _____ the hammer and killed all of the giants.

B Complete the sentences with the words below.

directions	period	questions	pause
surprised	marks	declarative	colon

1　A _____ sentence makes a statement about something.

2　We use interrogative sentences to ask _____.

3　An imperative sentence or a command gives orders or _____.

4　We use exclamatory sentences or exclamations when we are _____ or excited about something.

5　There are many kinds of punctuation _____ in English.

6　Most sentences end with a _____ (.).

7　A comma is like a _____ in the middle of a sentence.

8　Use a _____ (:) to list things or add explanations.

C

Write the correct word and the meaning in Chinese.

1  ▸ a Scandinavian pirate from the 8th to 10th centuries

_____

2  ▸ a flash of lightning that hits something

_____

3  ▸ someone who uses dishonest methods to get what they want

_____

4  Stop it! ▸ a sentence type that gives orders or directions

_____

5  ▸ a punctuation mark used to show that a person is speaking

_____

6  ▸ a fight between opposing forces

_____

D

Match each word with the correct definition and write the meaning in Chinese.

1 legend _____ ☐

2 refuse _____ ☐

3 dress up _____ ☐

4 play a trick on _____ ☐

5 declarative sentence; statement

_____ ☐

6 exclamatory sentence; exclamation

_____ ☐

7 imperative sentence; command

_____ ☐

8 punctuation mark _____ ☐

9 comma _____ ☐

10 question mark _____ ☐

a. to deceive somebody

b. to reject; to turn down

c. to put on a disguise or outfit

d. a sentence type that states something

e. a punctuation mark used for questions

f. an old story, often about brave people or adventures

g. a punctuation mark that is like a pause in the middle of a sentence

h. a mark such as a comma, colon, and question mark

i. a sentence type that gives orders or directions

j. a sentence type that shows surprise or excitement

Appreciating Artwork

Key Words

- art gallery
- exhibit
- masterpiece
- contrast
- sense of space
- realistic artist
- abstract artist
- foreground
- background
- middle ground
- appear
- perspective

Museums and art galleries exhibit all kinds of paintings. In many museums and art galleries, you can find great works of art called masterpieces.

What makes a masterpiece? There are many elements of painting. Many paintings have contrasts between light and shadows and bright colors and dark colors. Lines, shapes, and a sense of space are very important, too. Realistic artists and abstract artists use lines, shapes, and space differently.

Many paintings also have a foreground, background, and middle ground. The foreground is the objects that are closest to you. In the foreground, things are larger and more brightly colored than anything else in the painting. The background is the objects that are farthest from you. They appear smaller. The middle ground is those objects that are between the foreground and the background. This perspective makes paintings look more realistic.

All these different elements work together in every painting. Masters design the right balance of these elements in their works and make great works.

 What elements of painting can you see in the pictures?

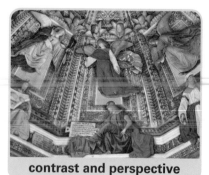
contrast and perspective

horizontal and vertical lines

a sense of space

Main Idea and Details

1 **What is the passage mainly about?**

a. Some famous masterpieces.   b. Important elements in paintings.
c. The importance of light and shadow.

2 **Many paintings have a foreground, background, and _____.**

a. middle ground   b. lower ground   c. upper ground

3 **What does perspective do?**

a. It lets artists use more colors.
b. It lets artists put shadows in their paintings.
c. It lets artists make their paintings more realistic.

4 **What does appear mean?**

a. Seem.   b. Become.   c. Create.

5 **Answer the questions.**

a. What do many paintings have contrasts between?

_____

b. What is the foreground? _____

c. What is the middle ground? _____

6 **Complete the outline**

Masterpieces

Elements	Perspective	Effects
• Contrasts between light and a_____ and bright colors and dark colors • Lines, shapes, and a sense of space are important.	• Makes paintings more b_____ • Foreground = closest objects • c_____ = farthest objects • Middle ground = objects between the foreground and background	• Different elements work together in paintings. • Can result in d_____

Vocabulary Builder

Write the correct word and the meaning in Chinese.

 ▸ an outstanding work of art

_____

 ▸ a room or building for the display of works of art

_____

 ▸ the front part of a scene or picture

_____

 ▸ a method of drawing a picture that shows distance and depth

_____

Creating Designs

Key Words

- **symmetry**
- **balance**
- **influence**
- **consider**
- **proportion**
- **symmetrical**
- **symmetric**
- **essential**
- **primary color**
- **secondary color**
- **complementary color**

When artists create art, they design their work by using lines, shapes, and colors. Symmetry and balance are two important features using lines and shapes.

The ancient Greeks created many beautiful paintings, buildings, and sculptures. Their art deeply influenced other artists in later years. The ancient Greeks considered balance and proportion to be the most important qualities of art. Ancient Greek buildings are carefully balanced and symmetrical. Symmetry and balance make something a better work of art. The Parthenon is the most famous symmetric building.

Color is another essential element of design. There are three primary colors: red, yellow, and blue. By mixing two primary colors together, we can make the three secondary colors. They are orange, green, and purple. Complementary colors are found opposite one another on the color wheel. Red and green are complementary colors that go together. So are blue and orange and yellow and purple.

✔ The Parthenon

a line of symmetry

Symmetry makes something a better work of art.

✔ Color Wheel

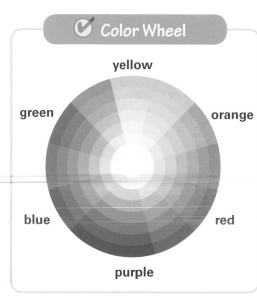

yellow

green

orange

blue

red

purple

✔ Complementary Colors

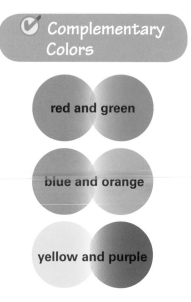

red and green

blue and orange

yellow and purple

Main Idea and Details

1   What is the passage mainly about?

a. Primary, secondary, and complementary colors.

b. The importance of symmetry, balance, and color.

c. The symmetry of the Parthenon.

2   Red, yellow, and blue are the three _____ colors.

a. primary   b. secondary   c. complementary

3   What are two features that use lines and shapes?

a. Symmetry and colors.   b. Balance and colors.   c. Symmetry and balance.

4   What does mixing mean?

a. Painting.   b. Combining.   c. Drawing.

5   Complete the sentences.

a. The art of the ancient _____ influenced other artists in later years.

b. A famous symmetric building is the _____.

c. Orange, green, and purple are the _____ colors.

6   Complete the outline.

Elements of Design

Symmetry and Balance

- Use lines and shapes
- Ancient Greek buildings are carefully
  a _____ and symmetrical.
- The b _____ = the most famous symmetric building

Colors

- c _____ colors = red, yellow, and blue
- Secondary colors = orange, green, and purple
- d _____ colors = those opposite other colors on the color wheel

Vocabulary Builder

Write the correct word and the meaning in Chinese.

 the quality of something that has two sides or halves that are the same

_____

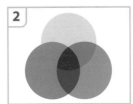 any of a set of colors from which all other colors may be derived

_____

 the ideal relationship between the size, shape, and position of different parts of something

 colors that are found opposite one another on the color wheel

_____

A World of Music
Elements of Music

Key Words

- **composer**
- **note**
- **rhythm**
- **pitch**
- **staff**
- **in a row**
- **musical scale**
- **major scale**
- **minor scale**
- **sharp note**
- **flat note**
- **step**
- **treble clef**
- **G clef**

When composers write music down, they use special marks called notes. The notes tell us the rhythm and the length of musical sounds. The composers also tell us the pitch—how high or low the notes should be—by placing the notes high or low on a staff.

When you sing or play these notes in a row, you are singing or playing a musical scale. There are seven main notes on a musical scale: A, B, C, D, E, F, and G. The notes on a musical scale all have a different pitch. There are a major scale of notes and a minor scale of notes.

There are also sharp and flat notes. A sharp note increases the pitch of a note by half a step. A flat note decreases the pitch of a note by half a step.

At the beginning of a staff, there is a special mark called a treble clef, or a G clef. The treble clef shows where the G note on the staff is.

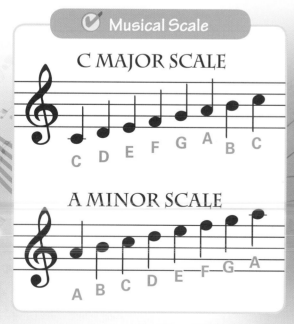

Main Idea and Details

1 **What is the passage mainly about?**

a. How to read music.   **b.** How sharp and flat notes differ.

c. What musical notes show.

2 **There are _____ main notes on a musical scale.**

a. seven   **b.** eight   **c.** nine

3 **What is another name for the G clef?**

a. The treble clef.   **b.** A minor.   **c.** G flat.

4 **What does increases mean?**

a. Lowers.   **b.** Raises.   **c.** Begins.

5 **According to the passage, which statement is true?**

a. There are both major and minor scales of notes.

b. The treble clef and G clef are not the same.

c. Notes only show the rhythm of the music.

6 **Complete the outline.**

Elements of Music

Musical Scale
- Has seven main notes = A, B, C, D, E, F, and G
- All have different pitches.
- There are ᵃ_____ and minor scales.

Musical Notes
- ᵇ_____ note = increases pitch by half a step
- Flat note = ᶜ_____ pitch by half a step

Special Mark
- Treble clef = ᵈ____ _____
- Is at the beginning of a staff
- Shows where the G note is

Vocabulary Builder

Write the correct word and the meaning in Chinese.

1 ▸ a person who writes music

_____

2 ▸ the five horizontal lines and the spaces between them on which music is written

_____

3 ▸ It increases the pitch of a note by half a step.

_____

4 ▸ It is also called the G clef.

_____

97

36

Key Words

• instruction
• legato
• staccato
• smoothly
• dynamics
• piano
• pianissimo
• mezzo piano
• moderately
• forte
• fortissimo
• mezzo forte
• Da Capo al Fine
• instruct
• repeat

Composers represent sounds by placing musical notes on a staff. Sometimes they give more specific instructions.

Two common instructions are legato and staccato. When musicians play legato, they should play the musical notes smoothly without breaks. But staccato should be played in the opposite way. When musicians play staccato, they should play each note by making a short, separate sound.

Also, the dynamics of the music are important. This refers to how loud or soft the music should be. The instructions are found in these letters: *p*, *pp*, *mp*, *f*, *ff*, and *mf*.

p means piano. This means a musician should play softly. *pp* means pianissimo, which is "very softly." And *mp* means mezzo piano, which is "moderately softly."

Sometimes musicians should play loudly. *f* means forte. This means a musician should play loudly. *ff* means fortissimo, which is "very loudly." And *mf* means mezzo forte, which is "moderately loudly."

Another instruction is *Da Capo al Fine*. *Da Capo* means "from the beginning." *Al Fine* means "to the end." *Da Capo al Fine* instructs the musician to repeat from the beginning up to the word *Fine*.

Smoothness

staccato   legato

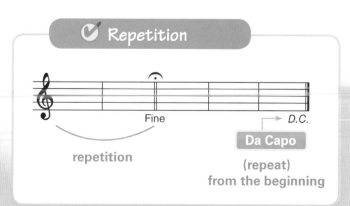

Repetition

Fine   D.C.

repetition

Da Capo
(repeat)
from the beginning

Main Idea and Details

1 **What is the main idea of the passage?**
   a. There are three stages of loudness that musicians can play.
   b. There are many instructions that musicians should follow when playing.
   c. *Da Capo al Fine* makes musicians repeat certain musical notes.

2 **Mezzo piano means** _____.
   a. softly   **b.** very softly   **c.** moderately softly

3 **What does fortissimo mean?**
   a. Loudly.   **b.** Very loudly.   **c.** Moderately loudly.

4 **What does separate mean?**
   a. Individual.   **b.** Loud.   **c.** Repeated.

5 **Complete the sentences.**
   a. _____ means that musicians should play smoothly.
   b. _____ means musicians should play short, separate sounds.
   c. *mf* stands for _____ _____.

6 **Complete the outline.**

Musical Instructions

Smoothness	Loudness or Softness	Repetition
• Legato = play smoothly with no breaks in between the notes • ᵃ _____ = play notes as short, separate sounds	• ᵇ _____ (*p*) = softly • Pianissimo (*pp*) = very softly • Mezzo piano (*mp*) = moderately softly • ᶜ _____ (*f*) = loudly • Fortissimo (*ff*) = very loudly • Mezzo forte (*mf*) = moderately loudly	• *Da Capo al Fine* = from the beginning up to the word *Fine* • Should ᵈ _____ the music in between the phrases

Vocabulary Builder

Write the correct word and the meaning in Chinese.

 ▸ moderately loudly
_____

 ▸ a musical instruction that tells you to play each note short and separately
_____

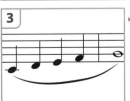 ▸ a musical instruction that tells you to play smoothly without breaks
_____

 ▸ very softly
_____

A Complete the sentences with the words below.

> balance   contrasts   foreground   essential
> exhibit   features   color wheel   proportion

1   Museums and art galleries _____ all kinds of paintings.

2   Many paintings have _____ between light and shadows and bright colors and dark colors.

3   Many paintings also have a _____, background, and middle ground.

4   Masters design the right _____ of these elements in their works and make great works.

5   Symmetry and balance are two important _____ using lines and shapes.

6   The ancient Greeks considered balance and _____ to be the most important qualities of art.

7   Color is another _____ element of design.

8   Complementary colors are found opposite one another on the _____ _____.

B Complete the sentences with the words below.

> staff   composers   scale   up to
> breaks   represent   softly   pitch

1   When _____ write music down, they use special marks called notes.

2   There are seven main notes on a musical _____: A, B, C, D, E, F, and G.

3   A flat note decreases the _____ of the note by half a step.

4   At the beginning of a _____, there is a special mark called a treble clef.

5   Composers _____ sounds by placing musical notes on a staff.

6   When musicians play legato, they should play the musical notes smoothly without _____.

7   *mp* means mezzo piano, which is "moderately _____."

8   *Da Capo al Fine* instructs the musician to repeat from the beginning _____ _____ the word *Fine*.

C

Write the correct word and the meaning in Chinese.

1 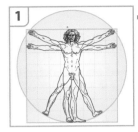 ▸ the ideal relationship between the size, shape, and position of different parts of something

_____

2  ▸ to display to the public

_____

3 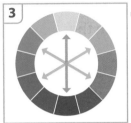 ▸ colors that are found opposite one another on the color wheel

_____

4 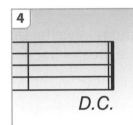 ▸ from the beginning

_____

D.C.

5  ▸ It has seven main notes: A, B, C, D, E, F, and G.

_____

6  ▸ It is also called the G clef.

_____

D

Match each word with the correct definition and write the meaning in Chinese.

1 contrast _____ ☐

2 perspective _____ ☐

3 influence _____ ☐

4 consider _____ ☐

5 essential _____ ☐

6 in a row _____ ☐

7 instruction _____ ☐

8 staccato _____ ☐

9 legato _____ ☐

10 moderately _____ ☐

a. to affect

b. fairly; properly

c. happening one after another

d. vital; important and necessary

e. to think about something very carefully

f. the differences in color or in light and darkness

g. information that tells you how to do something

h. a method of drawing a picture that shows distance and depth

i. a musical instruction that tells you to play smoothly without breaks

j. a musical instruction that tells you to play each note short and separately

Wrap-Up Test 3

A Write the correct word for each sentence.

> greater   fractions   thousandths   equal parts   imperative
> digits   equivalent   Yggdrasil   exclamatory   Ragnarök

1. Sometimes, we divide whole numbers into _____ _____.

2. Equivalent _____ have equal values but use different numbers.

3. When two fractions have the same denominator, the one with the _____ numerator is the greater fraction.

4. A decimal is a number with one or more _____ to the right of the decimal point.

5. The third place to the right of the decimal point is the _____ place.

6. You can say $\frac{1}{1000}$ is _____ to 0.001.

7. The Vikings believed that a giant "world tree" called _____ held up the universe.

8. Eventually, the giants would win this battle at _____.

9. An _____ sentence or a command gives orders or directions.

10. We use _____ sentences or exclamations when we are surprised or excited about something.

B Write the meanings of the words in Chinese.

1. denominator _____
2. numerator _____
3. mixed number _____
4. decimal point _____
5. ordinal number _____
6. cardinal number _____
7. digit _____
8. unit fraction _____
9. be equivalent to _____
10. confusing _____
11. individually _____
12. tenths place _____
13. thunderbolt _____
14. get married _____
15. interrogative sentence _____

16. quotes _____
17. battle _____
18. legend _____
19. refuse _____
20. dress up _____
21. play a trick on _____
22. declarative sentence _____
23. punctuation mark _____
24. exhibit _____
25. complementary colors _____
26. in a row _____
27. perspective _____
28. musical scale _____
29. moderately _____
30. G clef _____

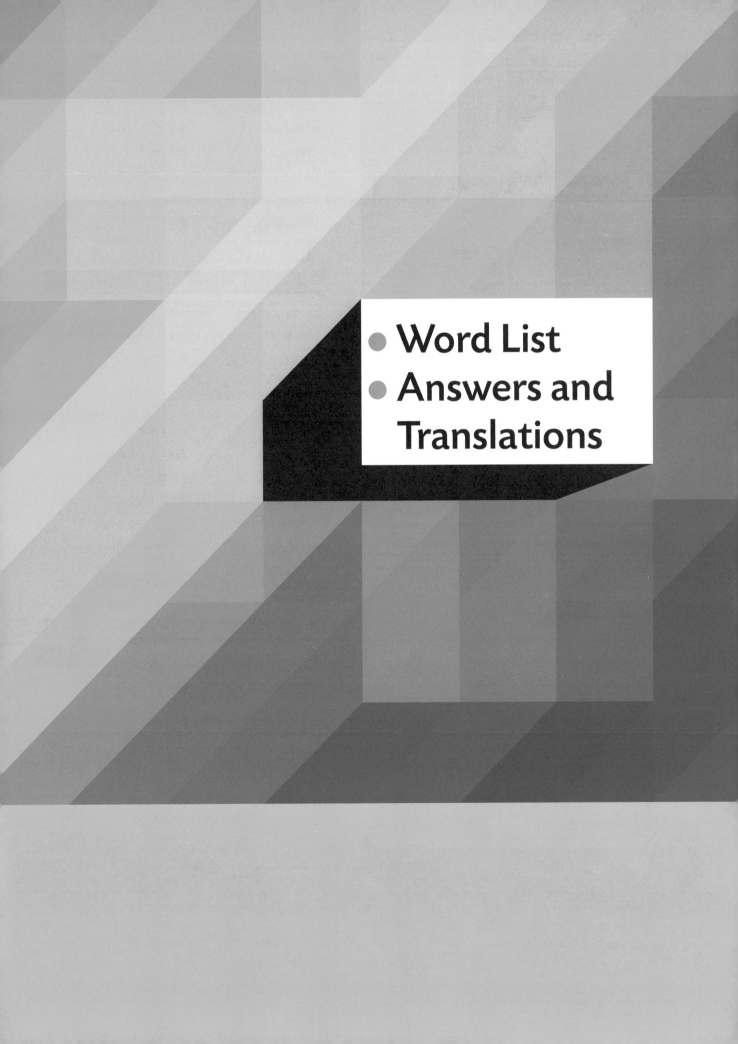

- Word List
- Answers and Translations

Word List

01 What Is a Globe?

1	**probably** (adv.)	或許
2	**globe** (n.)	地球儀
3	**model** (n.)	模型
4	**carefully** (adv.)	仔細地
5	**while** (conj.)	而；然而
6	**grid** (n.)	格子；座標方格
7	**imaginary** (a.)	虛構的；假想的
8	**line of latitude**	緯線
9	**line of longitude**	經線
10	**pass through**	通過
11	**North Pole**	北極
12	**South Pole**	南極

02 Understanding Hemispheres

1	**geographer** (n.)	地理學家
2	**hemisphere** (n.)	半球
3	**Northern Hemisphere**	北半球
4	**Southern Hemisphere**	南半球
5	**Western Hemisphere**	西半球
6	**Eastern Hemisphere**	東半球
7	**cover** (v.)	包含
8	**exactly** (adv.)	正好地；確切地
9	**equator** (n.)	赤道
10	**prime meridian**	本初子午線

03 The Environment of the West

1	**touch** (v.)	接觸；碰到
2	**coastline** (n.)	海岸線
3	**lush** (a.)	蒼翠茂盛的
4	**rugged** (a.)	崎嶇不平的
5	**a variety of**	各式各樣的

6	**extreme** (a.)	極端的
7	**active volcano**	活火山
8	**numerous** (a.)	眾多的；非常多的
9	**plenty of**	很多的
10	**fertile** (a.)	（土地）肥沃的
11	**valuable** (a.)	珍貴的
12	**throughout** (prep.)	遍及

04 The California Gold Rush

1	**carpenter** (n.)	木匠
2	**hire** (v.)	雇用
3	**mill** (n.)	磨坊
4	**flake** (n.)	小薄片
5	**secret** (n.)	祕密
6	**rumor** (n.)	謠言；傳聞
7	**rush** (v.) (n.)	湧現；衝；蜂擁前往
8	**gold rush**	淘金潮
9	**forty-niner** (n.)	四九人；淘金客
10	**empty-handed** (a.)	空手的；一無所有的
11	**bustling** (a.)	忙亂的；熙攘的
12	**explode** (v.)	激增；迅速擴大

05 The Environment of the Southwest

1	**be famous for**	以……著名
2	**climate** (n.)	氣候
3	**unusual** (a.)	不平常的；奇特的
4	**landform** (n.)	地形
5	**geographical** (a.)	地理學的；地理的
6	**feature** (n.)	特徵；特色
7	**run through**	穿過
8	**plateau** (n.)	高原
9	**canyon** (n.)	峽谷
10	**mesa** (n.)	臺地
11	**butte** (n.)	孤峰
12	**flow through**	流經

06 The Economy of the Southwest

1	**rainfall** (n.)	降雨；降雨量
2	**beneath** (prep.)	在……下面
3	**mine** (v.)	開採（礦物） *be mined
4	**petroleum** (n.)	石油
5	**nickname** (v.)	給……取綽號 *be nicknamed
6	**thriving** (a.)	興旺的；繁榮的
7	**oil industry**	石油工業
8	**petrochemical industry**	石油化學工業
9	**high-technology** (a.)	高科技的
10	**aircraft** (n.)	飛機；航空器總稱

07 The Environment of the Southeast

1	**region** (n.)	地區
2	**agriculture** (n.)	農業
3	**economy** (n.)	經濟
4	**location** (n.)	位置；地點
5	**crop** (n.)	農作物；莊稼
6	**growing season**	生長季
7	**source** (n.)	來源
8	**wetland** (n.)	溼地

08 The Civil Rights Movement

1	**1800s** (n.)	1800 年代
2	**plantation** (n.)	大農場
3	**cash crop**	經濟作物 （如菸草、棉花等）
4	**Southerner** (n.)	美國南方人
5	**meanwhile** (adv.)	同時
6	**slavery** (n.)	奴隸制度
7	**illegal** (a.)	非法的
8	**Northerner** (n.)	美國北方人
9	**Civil War**	美國內戰；南北戰爭 （1861–1865）

10	**segregation** (n.)	種族隔離
11	**restroom** (n.)	盥洗室；廁所
12	**Civil Rights Movement**	美國民權運動
13	**protest** (n.)	抗議
14	**demand** (v.)	要求
15	**equal treatment**	平等待遇
16	**guarantee** (v.)	擔保；保證

09 The Environment of the Northeast

1	**subregion** (n.)	（區以下的）分區
2	**bay** (n.)	海灣
3	**cape** (n.)	岬；海角
4	**Atlantic Coastal Plain**	大西洋沿岸平原
5	**trading center**	貿易中心
6	**mountain chain**	山脈
7	**mountain range**	山脈
8	**distinct** (a.)	明顯的；清楚的
9	**foliage** (n.)	葉子
10	**well-known** (a.)	著名的

10 The Leading Industries of the Northeast

1	**settler** (n.)	殖民者
2	**settle** (v.)	定居；移居於
3	**Industrial Revolution**	工業革命
4	**replace** (v.)	取代
5	**hand tool**	用手操作的簡易工具
6	**expand** (v.)	擴張；擴大
7	**financial** (a.)	金融的
8	**immigrant** (n.)	移民
9	**based on**	根據……；基於……
10	**metropolitan** (a.)	大都市的
11	**airport** (n.)	機場
12	**port** (n.)	港；港口

11 The Midwest Region

1	be made up of	由……組成
2	flat (a.)	平坦的
3	interior plain	內陸平原
4	mighty (a.)	巨大的;浩瀚的
5	Great Lakes	北美五大湖
6	breadbasket (n.)	糧倉;糧產區
7	countless (a.)	無數的
8	wheat (n.)	小麥
9	livestock (n.)	(總稱)家畜
10	automobile (n.)	汽車

12 The Mountain States

1	be covered with	被……覆蓋
2	majestic (a.)	雄偉的;壯觀的
3	Continental Divide	大陸分水嶺
4	peak (n.)	山峰
5	the Rockies	落磯山脈
6	inland (a.)	內陸的;內地的
7	mining (n.)	採礦;礦業
8	tourism (n.)	觀光業;旅遊業
9	outdoor (a.)	戶外的
10	recreation (n.)	消遣;娛樂
11	rafting (n.)	泛舟
12	attract (v.)	吸引
13	tourist (n.)	遊客;觀光客
14	quite (adv.)	很;相當

13 How Do Animals Grow?

1	life cycle	生命週期
2	fertilize (v.)	使受精
3	fertilized egg	受精卵
4	lay eggs	產卵;下蛋
5	nest (n.)	巢;窩
6	amphibian (n.)	兩棲動物
7	reptile (n.)	爬蟲類動物
8	hatch (v.)	孵化
9	female (n.)	雌性
10	go through	經歷
11	tiny (a.)	極小的;微小的
12	look like	看起來像……
13	rate (n.)	速度
14	fruit fly	果蠅

14 What Is Metamorphosis?

1	undergo (v.)	經歷 * 動詞三態 undergo-underwent-undergone
2	metamorphosis (n.)	(動物的)變態
3	butterfly (n.)	蝴蝶
4	moth (n.)	蛾
5	stage (n.)	階段;時期
6	caterpillar (n.)	毛毛蟲
7	larva (n.)	幼蟲;幼體
8	cocoon (n.)	繭
9	spin thread	吐絲
10	pupa (n.)	蛹

15 How Do Animals Respond to Changes?

1	environment (n.)	環境
2	respond to	對……作出反應
3	rely on	依賴;依靠
4	instinct (n.)	本能;天性
5	spider (n.)	蜘蛛
6	spin (v.)	(蜘蛛、蠶等)吐絲;結(繭) * 動詞三態 spin-spun-spun
7	spin a web	織網
8	adapt (v.)	適應
9	migrate (v.)	遷徙
10	hibernate (v.)	冬眠
11	barely (adv.)	幾乎不

12	migration (n.)	遷徙
13	hibernation (n.)	冬眠
14	behavior (n.)	行為；態度
15	young (n.)	幼獸；幼禽
16	cub (n.)	（熊、獅、虎等的）幼獸

16　Animal Adaptations for Survival

1	adaptation (n.)	適應
2	lizard (n.)	蜥蜴
3	tongue (n.)	舌頭
4	claw (n.)	爪
5	surroundings (n.)	環境
6	camouflage (n.)	偽裝；保護色
7	fur (n.)	毛皮
8	chameleon (n.)	變色龍
9	frequently (adv.)	常常；頻繁
10	still (a.)	靜止的；不動的
11	stay still	保持不動
12	predator (n.)	掠食者；食肉動物
13	mimicry (n.)	擬態
14	stonefish (n.)	石頭魚
15	spot (n.)	斑點
16	mimic (n.)	善於模仿者

17　What Changes Earth's Surface?

1	be caused by	起因於……
2	weathering (n.)	風化；風化作用
3	break down	分解
4	rushing (a.)	急衝的；急流的
5	weather (v.)	使風化
6	chemical (n.)	化學物質
7	erosion (n.)	侵蝕；侵蝕作用
8	weathered (a.)	被風化的
9	carry away	帶走；搬走
10	typically (adv.)	一般地；通常
11	glacier (n.)	冰河

12	blow away	吹走
13	mass (n.)	塊；團；堆
14	path (n.)	路徑；軌道

18　Fast Changes to Earth's Surface

1	earthquake (n.)	地震
2	volcano (n.)	火山
3	violent (a.)	激烈的；猛烈的
4	sudden (a.)	突然的；迅速的
5	crust (n.)	地殼
6	collapse (v.)	倒塌；瓦解
7	route (n.)	路線；路徑
8	stream (n.)	小河；溪流
9	instantly (adv.)	立即；馬上
10	erupt (v.)	噴出；爆發
11	lava (n.)	熔岩
12	build up	逐漸堆積

19　Our Solar System

1	solar system	太陽系
2	orbit (v.)	環繞（天體等的）軌道運行
3	planet (n.)	行星
4	moon (n.)	衛星
5	asteroid (n.)	小行星
6	inner planet	內行星
7	outer planet	外行星
8	farther away	離……更遠
9	rocky (a.)	岩石構成的；多岩石的
10	ring (n.)	環；環狀物
11	dust (n.)	塵埃；灰塵
12	asteroid belt	小行星帶

20　The Sun and Other Stars

1	celestial object	天體
2	other than	除了
3	comet (n.)	彗星

4	mixture (n.)	混合物
5	tail (n.)	尾巴；尾狀物
6	seem (v.)	看起來像
7	constellation (n.)	星座
8	the Big Dipper	北斗七星
9	the Little Dipper	小北斗星
10	galaxy (n.)	星系
11	universe (n.)	宇宙
12	contain (v.)	包含
13	on the edge of	在……邊緣
14	Milky Way Galaxy	銀河系

21 What Is Matter?

1	matter (n.)	物質
2	take up	佔據
3	describe (v.)	描述
4	property (n.)	特性
5	tell . . . apart	分辨……
6	element (n.)	元素
7	substance (n.)	物質
8	hydrogen (n.)	氫
9	oxygen (n.)	氧
10	nitrogen (n.)	氮
11	helium (n.)	氦
12	compound (n.)	化合物
13	combination (n.)	結合
14	atom (n.)	原子
15	particle (n.)	粒子
16	molecule (n.)	分子

22 Changes in Matter

1	physical change	物理變化
2	chemical change	化學變化
3	physically (adv.)	物理地
4	state (n.)	形態
5	solid state	固態

6	liquid state	液態
7	gas state	氣態
8	solution (n.)	溶液；溶劑
9	pour (v.)	倒；灌
10	stir (v.)	攪動；攪拌
11	dissolve (v.)	溶解
12	involve (v.)	包含；牽涉
13	separate (a.)	不同的
14	combine (v.)	結合

23 Taking Care of Our Bodies

1	get sick	生病
2	catch a cold	感冒
3	flu (n.)	流行性感冒
4	disease (n.)	疾病
5	illness (n.)	疾病
6	germ (n.)	微生物；病菌
7	virus (n.)	病毒
8	bacteria (n.)	細菌
9	shot (n.)	注射
10	medicine (n.)	藥；內服藥
11	get better	逐漸痊癒
12	habit (n.)	嗜好；習慣
13	hygiene (n.)	衛生
14	exercise (v.) (n.)	運動
15	balanced (a.)	均衡的
16	diet (n.)	飲食
17	unhealthy (a.)	不健康的
18	junk food	垃圾食物

24 The Six Nutrients

1	nutrient (n.)	營養物
2	function (n.)	運作
3	properly (adv.)	恰當地；正確地
4	carbohydrate (n.)	碳水化合物
5	fat (n.)	脂肪；脂質

6	protein (n.)	蛋白質	
7	vitamin (n.)	維生素;維他命	
8	mineral (n.)	礦物質	
9	starch (n.)	澱粉	
10	repair (v.)	恢復;修補	
11	dairy product	乳製品	
12	remove (v.)	移動;搬移	
13	waste (n.)	廢物	
14	normal (a.)	正常的;標準的	

25 Fractions

1	whole number	整數
2	equal part	等分;均分
3	fraction (n.)	分數
4	numerator (n.)	分子
5	denominator (n.)	分母
6	represent (v.)	表示
7	mixed number	帶分數
8	equivalent (a.)	相等的;等值的
9	equivalent fraction	等值分數
10	unit fraction	單位分數

26 Understanding Fractions

1	name (v.)	陳述;指定
2	shaded (a.)	色彩較暗的
3	compare (v.)	比較
4	order (v.)	點菜;訂購
5	slice (v.)	切;把……切成薄片
6	take (v.)	拿;取

27 Understanding Decimals

1	decimal (n.) (a.)	小數;小數的
2	decimal point	小數點
3	digit (n.)	數字
4	tenths place	十分位
5	hundredths place	百分位

6	thousandths place	千分位
7	be equivalent to	與……相等的
8.	equivalent decimal	等值小數

28 Reading and Writing Fractions and Decimals

1	confusing (a.)	令人困惑的
2	cardinal number	基數
3	ordinal number	序數
4	out of . . .	從……裡
5	individually (adv.)	分別地;逐個地
6	zero (n.)	零

29 Norse Mythology

1	Norse (a.)	古斯堪地那維亞的
2	mythology (n.)	神話
3	Viking (n.)	維京人
4	Norseman (n.)	古斯堪地那維亞人
5	ancient (a.)	古代的
6	legend (n.)	傳說;傳奇故事
7	chief god	主神
8	raven (n.)	渡鴉
9	thunder (n.)	雷
10	swing (v.)	擺動

* 動詞三態
swing-swung-swung

11	mighty (a.)	巨大的
12	hammer (n.)	鐵鎚
13	thunderbolt (n.)	雷電
14	trickster (n.)	(神話中的)惡作劇精靈;騙子
15	battle (n.)	戰鬥;戰役

30 Loki the Trickster

1	return (v.)	歸還
2	marry (v.)	娶;和……結婚
3	refuse (v.)	拒絕

4	**suggestion** (n.)	建議；提議
5	**get married**	結婚
6	**play a trick on**	捉弄……；對……惡作劇
7	**dress up**	裝扮
8	**servant** (n.)	僕人
9	**in disguise**	偽裝；假扮
10	**wedding party**	婚禮
11	**lift** (v.)	舉起；抬起
12	**veil** (n.)	面紗；面罩
13	**ceremony** (n.)	典禮；儀式
14	**grab** (v.)	抓住

31 What Kind of Sentence Is It?

1	**declarative sentence**	直述句
2	**statement** (n.)	陳述句；陳述
3	**interrogative sentence**	疑問句
4	**question** (n.)	問句；問題
5	**imperative sentence**	祈使句
6	**command** (n.)	命令
7	**exclamatory sentence**	感嘆句
8	**exclamation** (n.)	驚嘆；感嘆；感嘆句
9	**end with**	以……結束
10	**question mark**	問號
11	**subject** (n.)	主詞
12	**exclamation point**	驚嘆號
13	**be surprised**	感到驚訝
14	**amazing** (a.)	驚人的；令人吃驚的

32 Punctuation Marks

1	**punctuation mark**	標點符號
2	**situation** (n.)	情況
3	**comma** (n.)	逗號
4	**pause** (n.)	暫停
5	**list** (v.)	列舉

6	**dash** (n.)	破折號
7	**quotes** (n.)	引號
8	**hyphen** (n.)	連字號

33 Appreciating Artwork

1	**museum** (n.)	博物館
2	**art gallery**	美術館；畫廊
3	**exhibit** (v.)	陳列；展覽
4	**masterpiece** (n.)	名作；名著
5	**element** (n.)	成分；要素
6	**contrast** (n.)	對比；對照
7	**sense of space**	空間感
8	**realistic** (a.)	現實主義的
9	**abstract** (a.)	抽象主義的
10	**foreground** (n.)	前景
11	**background** (n.)	背景
12	**farthest** (a.)	（距離、時間上）最遠的
13	**appear** (v.)	似乎；看來好像
14	**perspective** (n.)	透視畫法

34 Creating Designs

1	**symmetry** (n.)	對稱
2	**balance** (n.)	平衡；均衡
3	**feature** (n.)	特徵；特色
4	**sculpture** (n.)	雕刻品；雕像
5	**influence** (v.)	影響
6	**in later years**	往後幾年裡
7	**consider** (v.)	認為
8	**proportion** (n.)	比例
9	**symmetrical** (a.)	對稱的
10	**symmetric** (a.)	對稱的
11	**essential** (a.)	基本的；必要的
12	**primary color**	原色
13	**secondary color**	二次色
14	**opposite** (prep.)	在……的對面
15	**color wheel**	色環；色輪

16 **complementary color**　互補色

35　Elements of Music

1　**composer** (n.)　作曲者；作曲家
2　**note** (n.)　音符
3　**pitch** (n.)　音高
4　**staff** (n.)　五線譜
5　**in a row**　接連地；連續不斷地
6　**musical scale**　音階
7　**major scale**　大調音階
8　**minor scale**　小調音階
9　**sharp note**　升記號
10　**flat note**　降記號
11　**treble clef**　高音譜號
12　**G clef**　G 譜號

36　Musical Instructions

1　**represent** (v.)　表現；描述
2　**specific** (a.)　明確的；詳盡的
3　**instruction** (n.)　指示；說明
4　**legato** (n.) (adv.)　連奏；連奏地
5　**staccato** (n.) (adv.)　斷奏；斷奏地
6　**in the opposite way**　以相反的方式
7　**moderately** (adv.)　適度地；中等地
8　**loudly** (adv.)　大聲地
9　**repeat** (v.)　重複
10　**up to**　一直到

Answers and Translations

01 What Is a Globe? 何謂地球儀？

環顧教室四周，你可能會看到一個地球儀。什麼是地球儀呢？地球儀是用來展示地球樣貌的地球模型。

地球儀是地圖的一種，上面顯示地球上所有的陸地和海洋。你只要轉動地球儀，就可以看到七大洲和五大洋。但是，地球儀所顯示的並不僅止於此。

仔細看看地球儀，上頭有很多線條，有的是水平線，有的是垂直線。這些方格上面的線條，是兩組環繞地球的假想線。

東西向環繞的水平線叫緯線，南北向環繞的垂直線叫經線。經線通過北極和南極。我們只要知道一個地方的經緯度，就可以知道它在地球儀上的確切位置。

- **Main Idea and Details**
1 **(b)**　　2 **(a)**　　3 **(c)**　　4 **(b)**
5 a. **model**　　b. **north**　　c. **latitude**
6 a. **earth**　　b. **continents**　　c. **horizontal**　　d. **Longitude**
- **Vocabulary Builder**
1 **grid** 格子；座標方格　　2 **globe** 地球儀
3 **line of latitude** 緯線　　4 **line of longitude** 經線

02 Understanding Hemispheres 認識地球半球

地理學家將地球分為四個半球，分別是北半球、南半球、西半球和東半球。hemi 這個字就是「二分之一」的意思，一個半球所涵蓋的範圍就是二分之一的地球。

地球以赤道為界，分為南北半球。赤道是地球正中間的緯線，赤道以北是北半球，亞洲、歐洲和北美洲位於北半球。赤道以南是南半球，部分非洲地區、南美洲、澳洲和南極洲都位於南半球。

地球以本初子午線為界，分為東西半球。本初子午線是一條由北極延伸至南極的經線，正好通過英國的格林威治。南、北美洲都位於西半球，歐洲、亞洲、非洲、澳洲和南極洲則位於東半球。

- **Main Idea and Details**
1 **(c)**　　2 **(b)**　　3 **(b)**　　4 **(c)**　　5 **(c)**
6 a. **equator**　b. **Antarctica**　c. **South America**　d. **Australia**
- **Vocabulary Builder**
1 **divide** 分；劃分　　2 **lie** 位於
3 **equator** 赤道　　4 **prime meridian** 本初子午線

03 The Environment of the West 美國西部地理環境

美國西部各州皆鄰近太平洋，包含加州、內華達州、奧勒岡州和華盛頓州。阿拉斯加州和夏威夷州也位於西部地區，但不與其他州接鄰。

美國西部各州以濱太平洋的綿長海岸線而聞名，其蒼翠繁茂的森林、炎熱的沙漠和崎嶇的高山亦聞名遐邇。

西部地區涵蓋多種氣候型態。內華達州和加州擁有許多沙漠，加州的死亡谷是世界上最乾燥的地方之一。然而，也有許多地方降雨豐沛。事實上，奧勒岡州和華盛頓州甚至有雨林分布。西部的氣候有時非常極端。太平洋沿岸常有地震發生，阿拉斯加、夏威夷和華盛頓州境內則有活火山。

西部地區富含天然資源，豐富的肥沃土壤利於農業發展，森林也為全國各地提供大量的珍貴木材。西部地區亦可見高山與縱谷，喀斯開山脈和內華達山脈皆位於西部地區。

- **Main Idea and Details**
1 **(a)**　　2 **(a)**　　3 **(b)**　　4 **(b)**
5 a. **California, Nevada, Oregon, Washington, Alaska, and Hawaii are in the West.**
　b. **Earthquakes often strike along the Pacific coast.**
　c. **Some rain forests are located in Oregon and Washington.**
6 a. **Hawaii**　　b. **deserts**　　c. **fertile**　　d. **forests**
- **Vocabulary Builder**
1 **lush** 蒼翠茂盛的　　2 **rugged** 崎嶇不平的
3 **strike** 侵襲　　4 **coast** 海岸；沿岸地區

04 The California Gold Rush 美國加州淘金熱

詹姆士・馬歇爾是受雇於加州薩特磨坊的木匠。1848 年時，他正在美國河岸為約翰・薩特建造一座磨坊。有一天，馬歇爾正在造磨坊時，在河中發現了一些閃亮的金屬片。雖然他和約翰・薩特試圖保守這個祕密，消息卻還是很快傳開了，於是人人皆知加州有黃金。

美國東部居民在數月後才得知這個消息，但是沒多久就有數以千計的淘金客前往加州。截至 1849 年，已有超過 8 萬人湧入加州，皆為金礦慕名而來，形成一波「加州淘金熱」。這些淘金礦工是在 1849 年來到加州，因此也被稱為「49 人」。有些人發現金礦而致富，但也有人一無所獲、空手而回。

在 1800 年代早期，美國西部還只是人口稀少的平靜地區。然而，金礦的發現卻讓西部充滿了熙攘繁忙的城市，人口也隨之暴增，而加州則在 1850 年正式成為美國的一州。

- **Main Idea and Details**
1 **(b)**　　2 **(a)**　　3 **(b)**　　4 **(c)**
5 a. **secret**　　b. **forty-niners**　　c. **1850**
6 a. **Rumors**　　b. **empty**　　c. **population**　　d. **state**

• **Vocabulary Builder**

1 **miner** 礦工　　　　2 **discovery** 發現；被發現的事物
3 **gold rush** 淘金潮　　4 **bustling** 忙亂的；熙攘的

Vocabulary Review 1

A

1 **looks**　　　　　　2 **horizontal**
3 **circle**　　　　　　4 **pass through**
5 **half**　　　　　　　6 **equator**
7 **lies**　　　　　　　8 **Western**

B

1 **coastlines**　　　　2 **variety**
3 **extreme**　　　　　4 **fertile**
5 **hired**　　　　　　6 **flakes**
7 **secret**　　　　　　8 **discovery**

C

1 **secret** 祕密　　　　　2 **line of latitude** 緯線
3 **hemisphere** 半球　　　4 **prime meridian** 本初子午線
5 **rugged** 崎嶇不平的　　6 **active volcano** 活火山

D

1 模型 **b**　　　　　　2 經線 **i**
3 地理學家 **f**　　　　　4 本初子午線 **h**
5 木匠 **g**　　　　　　6 蒼翠茂盛的 **d**
7 極端的 **c**　　　　　8 淘金潮 **j**
9 湧現；衝 **a**　　　　10 忙亂的；熙攘的 **e**

05 The Environment of the Southwest
美國西南部地理環境

美國西南部以晴朗氣候和奇特地貌而聞名，亞歷桑那州、新墨西哥州、奧克拉荷馬州和德州是西南部的四個州。

西南部地區大多乾燥酷熱，因此許多土地為沙漠所覆蓋。彩繪沙漠和索諾蘭沙漠皆位於亞歷桑那州。

不過，西南部仍有著千姿百態的地理景觀。落磯山脈橫亙此區，還有許多高原、峽谷、臺地和孤峰。科羅拉多高原是美國西南部的主要高原，尤以峽谷著稱，大峽谷即為其一。

雖然西南部許多土地乾涸，仍有幾條主要河川位於此區。科羅拉多河流經亞歷桑那州，並且創造了大峽谷。位於德州和墨西哥邊境的格蘭特河，也是此區的主要河川。

• **Main Idea and Details**

1 **(b)**　　　2 **(c)**　　　3 **(a)**　　　4 **(a)**
5 a. **They are the Painted Desert and the Sonoran Desert.**
　 b. **The Rocky Mountains are in the Southwest.**
　 c. **The Colorado River and the Rio Grande River are two major rivers.**
6 a. **Texas**　　b. **Deserts**　　c. **buttes**　　d. **between**

• **Vocabulary Builder**

1 **geographical** 地理的　　2 **plateau** 高原
3 **butte** 孤峰　　　　　　4 **mesa** 臺地

06 The Economy of the Southwest
美國西南部經濟

雖然美國西南部雨量稀少，卻饒富天然資源。其中兩種最重要的資源蘊藏於地底，即礦藏和石油。

德州、亞歷桑那州和新墨西哥州是煤、銅、銀和鈾等礦區。德州和奧克拉荷馬州是最大的兩個石油產區。石油是油礦的普遍稱呼，由於非常珍貴，因而也被稱為「黑金」。「黑金」帶動了西南部的經濟振興，全國各地都在使用這裡開採的石油。

今日，西南部各州的經濟蓬勃發展，每年都有越來越多的美國人，受到此區的多元工業所吸引而移居至此。

西南部的石油工業持續強盛，石化工業的規模也非常龐大。貿易和高科技產業，如飛機製造，亦促進了西南部的發展。

• **Main Idea and Details**

1 **(b)**　　　2 **(c)**　　　3 **(a)**　　　4 **(b)**
5 a. **ground**　　b. **moving**　　c. **aircraft**
6 a. **Coal**　b. **Oklahoma**　c. **black gold**　d. **petrochemical**

• **Vocabulary Builder**

1 **black gold** 黑金　　　　2 **mine** 開採（礦物）
3 **thriving** 興旺的；繁榮的　4 **rich in** 富含；有很多……

07 The Environment of the Southeast
美國東南部地理環境

美國東南部是全國最大的地區之一，包括了 12 州：阿拉巴馬州、阿肯色州、佛羅里達州、喬治亞州、肯塔基州、路易斯安那州、密西西比州、北卡羅萊納州、南卡羅萊納州、田納西州、維吉尼亞州、西維吉尼亞州。

農業是東南部的經濟重心，因其地理位置，一年中多為溫暖氣候。豐沛的雨量和肥沃的土壤利於耕種各種農作物，同時由於生長季長，東南部也因此成為許多蔬果的產區。

東南部地區有許多河川、湖泊和溼地。密西西比河流經美國東南部的西區，數百年來一直是美國的旅遊和貿易中心。

此地區還有許多珍貴的天然資源，全國多數的煤礦來自西維吉尼亞州和肯塔基州。

• **Main Idea and Details**

1 **(b)**　　2 **(b)**　　3 **(c)**　　4 **(b)**　　5 **(c)**
6 a. **West Virginia**　b. **Mississippi**　c. **rainfall**　d. **resources**

• **Vocabulary Builder**

1 **agriculture** 農業　　　　2 **growing season** 生長季
3 **crop** 農作物；莊稼　　　4 **wetland** 溼地

08 The Civil Rights Movement
美國黑人民權運動

1800 年代時，美國東南部的大多數人民以務農維生，那裡有許多的大農場。農場主人種植經濟作物以販賣圖利，棉花即為當時最重要的經濟作物。

由於農場需要大量勞工，因此許多南方人擁有非洲黑人當農奴，這些黑奴的生活非常艱苦。

而在當時，奴隸制度在北方各州多屬非法，許多北方人認為奴隸制度是錯誤的，必須被廢除。在 1860 年代時，美國北方和南方展開了南北戰爭，北方戰勝，奴隸制度因而被禁止。

然而，大部分美國南方的黑人仍然無法和白人公民享有平權，種族隔離行為處處可見。黑人無法與白人一起生活、工作，甚至不能共用廁所。

到了 1950 年代，美國黑人民權運動展開。馬丁‧路德‧金恩博士成為其中一位領袖，他帶領抗爭，主張人人生而平等。終於在 1964 年通過《民權法案》，保障每個人都能受到平等的待遇。

- Main Idea and Details

1 (c)　　2 (c)　　3 (b)　　4 (a)

5 a. **Cotton was an important cash crop.**
　b. **The North and South fought the Civil War.**
　c. **It began in the 1950s.**

6 a. **slaves**　b. **rights**　c. **whites**　d. **Movement**　e. **passed**

- Vocabulary Builder

1 **Civil War** 美國內戰；南北戰爭　　2 **protest** 抗議；反對

3 **slavery** 奴隸制度　　　　　　　　4 **segregation** 種族隔離

Vocabulary Review 2

A

1 **climate**　　　　　2 **located**
3 **plateau**　　　　　4 **major**
5 **rainfall**　　　　　6 **mined**
7 **nicknamed**　　　　8 **thriving**

B

1 **location**　　　　　2 **growing**
3 **flows**　　　　　　4 **throughout**
5 **Plantation**　　　　6 **slaves**
7 **Civil War**　　　　8 **equally**

C

1 **plateau** 高原　　　　　2 **canyon** 峽谷
3 **butte** 孤峰　　　　　　4 **mine** 開採（礦物）
5 **plantation** 大農場　　　6 **cash crop** 經濟作物，如菸草、棉花等

D

1 地形 **i**　　　　　　2 開採（礦物）**f**
3 興旺的；繁榮的 **a**　4 飛機；航空器總稱 **d**
5 降雨；降雨量 **j**　　6（土地）肥沃的 **b**
7 農作物；莊稼 **e**　　8 溼地 **h**
9 奴隸制度 **c**　　　　10 種族隔離 **g**

09 The Environment of the Northeast
美國東北部地理環境

美國東北部可分為兩個區域：新英格蘭和中大西洋地區。新英格蘭包括緬因州、新罕布夏州、麻薩諸塞州、佛蒙特州、羅德島州和康乃迪克州。中大西洋地區包括紐約州、賓夕法尼亞州、紐澤西州、德拉威州和馬里蘭州。

大西洋沿岸有許多海灣、岬角和島嶼，麻薩諸塞州的鱈魚角是東北部最著名的岬角之一。大西洋沿岸平原有許多深港，有海港的城市佔地利之便，容易與其他地區和國家貿易。因此，東北部的城市如紐約、波士頓和費城，已成為重要的貿易中心。

東北部也有許多山脈，阿帕拉契山脈幾乎綿亙此區各州。阿帕拉契山脈是世界上最古老的山脈之一。

東北部各州有明顯的四季之分，夏熱而冬冷。到了秋天，色彩繽紛的樹葉是東北森林的一大特色。

- Main Idea and Details

1 (b)　　2 (a)　　3 (a)　　4 (c)

5 a. **subregions**　b. **Cape Cod**　c. **foliage**
6 a. **Maryland**　b. **harbors**　c. **seasons**　d. **fall**

- Vocabulary Builder

1 **subregion**（區以下的）分區　　2 **mountain range** 山脈

3 **foliage** 葉子　　　　　　　　　4 **cape** 岬；海角

10 The Leading Industries of the Northeast
美國東北部的主要工業

許多來自歐洲的首批移民定居在美國東北部，並以務農為主。在 1700 年代中期，多數美國人在農場上居住和生活。然而，從 1700 年代晚期到 1800 年代中期，工業革命改變了人們的生活方式。

機器在當時取代了手工具，商品的製造速度變快，新興工業出現，經濟擴張，沒多久工廠變得跟農場一樣重要。

當工業革命擴散至全國各地，東北部便成為美國的製造業中心。新興的工廠和企業全都需要大量工人，因此越來越多移民來到紐約尋找新契機。

以土地面積來說，東北部是美國最小的一區。然而，此區在許多方面都具有舉足輕重的地位。東北部比其他地區擁有更多都會區。這裡也是教育重鎮，優秀學校如哈佛大學、耶魯大學和麻省理工學院都位於此地。紐約市更是全球主要的金融中心。此外，遍佈東北各地的機場和海港，亦有助於進出口為數龐大的貨物。

- Main Idea and Details

1 (b)　　2 (c)　　3 (a)　　4 (a)　　5 (b)

6 a. **way**　b. **manufacturing**　c. **financial**　d. **export**

- Vocabulary Builder

1 **Industrial Revolution** 工業革命

2 **hand tool** 用手操作的簡易工具

3 **metropolitan area** 都會區

4 **export** 出口

11 The Midwest Region 美國中西部地區

美國中西部地區包括 12 個州：俄亥俄州、印第安那州、密西根州、威斯康辛州、伊利諾州、明尼蘇達州、愛荷華州、密蘇里州、北達科塔州、南達科塔州、內布拉斯加州和堪薩斯州。

中西部地區的地勢低平，主要地形為兩個內陸平原：中央平原和北美大平原。此外，有三條重要河川流經此區，分別是浩瀚的密西西比河、俄亥俄河和密蘇里河。五大湖區也位於中西部。

中西部的兩個主要工業為農業和製造業，並素有「美國的糧倉」之稱。這裡有著數不盡的麥田、玉米田和其他作物田地。同時，中西部的許多農夫飼養豬隻、牛隻和其他家畜，美國大部分的糧食都產自此地。

中西部也是製造業中心。亨利・福特在密西根的底特律開創汽車事業，底特律很快就成為世界汽車中心，許多大車商都在這裡設廠。中西部各地亦有許多其他工業。

- Main Idea and Details
1 (c)　　　2 (a)　　　3 (c)　　　4 (b)　　　5 (a)
6 a. Michigan　　b. Plain　　c. Lakes　　d. manufacturing

- Vocabulary Builder
1 interior 內地的；內陸的　　2 breadbasket 糧倉；糧產區
3 raise 飼養　　4 livestock （總稱）家畜

12 The Mountain States 美國山區

愛達荷州、蒙大拿州、懷俄明州、科羅拉多州和猶他州是美國山區的五個州。

美國山區被高山所覆蓋，巍峨的落磯山脈綿互此區各州，峰峰相連由北而南構成了大陸分水嶺。這些州也擁有許多河川和廣大的森林。大鹽湖位於猶他州北部，是西半球最大的內陸鹹水湖。

礦業是美國山區最重要的工業之一，落磯山脈蘊含豐富的金屬和礦物資源，如銅和天然氣。

觀光業是美國山區另一項重要行業，諸如滑雪、登山和泛舟等戶外休閒活動，每年都吸引數千名遊客前來此地。

美國山區的人口稀少，少有城市超過五萬人口。丹佛和鹽湖城是此區最大的城市。

- Main Idea and Details
1 (b)　　　2 (c)　　　3 (a)　　　4 (b)
5 a. Rocky　　b. Mining　　c. cities
6 a. Utah　　b. Continental　　c. metals　　d. recreation

- Vocabulary Builder
1 peak 山峰　　2 Continental Divide 大陸分水嶺
3 recreation 消遣；娛樂　　4 inland 內地的；內陸的

Vocabulary Review 3

A
1 subregions　　　　2 Along
3 harbors　　　　4 Appalachians
5 distinct　　　　6 Industrial
7 replaced　　　　8 metropolitan

B
1 made up　　　　2 manufacturing
3 raise　　　　4 became
5 runs　　　　6 inland
7 industries　　　　8 Outdoor

C
1 import 進口　　　2 mountain range 山脈
3 foliage 葉子　　　4 hand tool 用手操作的簡易工具
5 livestock （總稱）家畜　　6 majestic 雄偉的；壯觀的

D
1 著名的 c　　　　2 工業革命 j
3 取代 a　　　　4 金融的 g
5 巨大的；浩瀚的 b　　6 糧倉；糧產區 f
7 無數的 d　　　　8 山峰 h
9 採礦；礦業 i　　　10 吸引 e

Wrap-Up Test 1

A
1 globe　　　　2 longitude
3 hemispheres　　　4 landforms
5 nicknamed　　　6 growing
7 cash crops　　　8 metropolitan
9 Revolution　　　10 Rockies

B
1 緯線　　　　2 半球
3 赤道　　　　4 經線
5 本初子午線　　　6 地形
7 高原　　　　8 石油
9 興旺的；繁榮的　　10 臺地
11 大農場　　　　12 經濟作物（如菸草、棉花等）
13 岬；海角　　　14 山脈
15 種族隔離　　　16 降雨；降雨量
17 （土地）肥沃的　　18 農作物；莊稼
19 溼地　　　　20 奴隸制度
21 葉子　　　　22 工業革命
23 取代　　　　24 金融的
25 蒼翠茂盛的　　　26 極端的
27 忙亂的；熙攘的　　28 崎嶇不平的
29 大都市的　　　30 明顯的；清楚的

13 How Do Animals Grow?
動物如何成長？

每種動物都有生命週期。動物的種類繁多，因此也有著各種生命週期。

幾乎所有動物都由受精卵而來。許多鳥類會築巢下蛋，魚類和兩棲動物在水中產卵，爬蟲類動物也會產卵，並在雌性體外孵化。有些動物如青蛙和昆蟲，在孵化之後，要經歷一串完整的身體變化，才會成為成體。

哺乳動物在母親體內展開生命，牠們從母體內的受精卵開始發育，出生時即是活體。牠們出生時小小的，但外貌與成體相似。牠們隨著成長而變大，容貌也有所改變。不過，牠們不會經歷其他重大變化，這種成長過程被稱為直接發育。

動物的成長速度也各有不同，果蠅約十天即可變為成蟲，狗則要大約三歲才算成犬。

- **Main Idea and Details**

1 **(c)**　　　2 **(b)**　　　3 **(a)**　　　4 **(c)**

5 a. **nests**　　b. **change**　　c. **ten**

6 a. **amphibians**　　b. **complete**　　c. **live**　　d. **adult**

- **Vocabulary Builder**

1 **life cycle** 生命週期　　　2 **lay** 下蛋；產卵

3 **hatch** 孵化　　　4 **direct development** 直接發育

14 What Is Metamorphosis? 何謂變態？

動物在生長過程中會經歷變化。有些動物如魚和人類，隨著年齡增加只會長大。然而，有些動物卻會經歷重大的生命週期變化，稱為「變態」。

「變態」是指動物在身體形態上的重大改變。蝴蝶和蛾會經歷變態過程，青蛙等大部分的兩棲動物也會經歷變態。

完整的變態過程分為四個階段，讓我們仔細來瞧瞧蝴蝶的變態過程。

首先，蝴蝶產下受精卵。第二階段時，小毛毛蟲，也就是蝴蝶的幼蟲，從卵中孵化。毛毛蟲開始覓食並且成長，準備進入下一階段。到了第三階段，牠會製作一個繭。繭是毛毛蟲吐絲用來裹住自己的硬殼，於是牠成為一個蛹。牠會在繭中經歷變態過程。最後來到第四階段，成蝶破繭而出。

- **Main Idea and Details**

1 **(a)**　　2 **(a)**　　3 **(b)**　　4 **(b)**　　5 **(c)**

6 a. **Butterflies**　b. **Hatches**　c. **pupa**　d. **cocoon**

- **Vocabulary Builder**

1 **metamorphosis**（動物的）變態　　2 **larva** 幼蟲

3 **cocoon** 繭　　　4 **pupa** 蛹

15 How Do Animals Respond to Changes?
動物如何適應環境變化？

環境經常改變，動物會用各種不同方式來應付這些環境變化。

動物通常仰賴牠們的本能。本能是動物與生俱來的能力，舉例來說，牠們可能知道哪些動物具有威脅性，哪些則無害。此外，蜘蛛生來就知道如何結網捕食。

許多動物藉由遷徙或冬眠來適應寒冬。當天氣逐漸寒冷，有些動物會遷徙到溫暖的地方去覓食。有些動物如熊類，則會找地方冬眠。冬眠中的動物由於身體機能幾乎停止運作，不需要太多能量，因此冬季並不需要進食。遷徙跟冬眠都是動物的本能行為。

有些動物同時也有「習得行為」。哺乳動物通常由母親教授這些「習得行為」給孩子，牠們會教孩子如何覓食和自衛。幼熊大約在六個月大時學習爬樹，大多數的人類行為也是經由學習而來。

- **Main Idea and Details**

1 **(c)**　　　2 **(a)**　　　3 **(b)**　　　4 **(b)**

5 a. **It is an example of instinctive behavior.**
　b. **They migrate in search of food.**
　c. **Bears hibernate.**

6 a. **born**　　b. **search**　　c. **young**　　d. **protect**

- **Vocabulary Builder**

1 **instinct** 本能；天性　　　2 **migrate** 遷徙

3 **learned behavior** 習得行為　　　4 **hibernate** 冬眠

16 Animal Adaptations for Survival
動物適者生存

動物為了生存，有著各種適應方式。適應可能表現在一種動物經遺傳演化而來的身體部位或行為上。

青蛙和蜥蜴擁有長舌以便捕捉昆蟲。獅子的速度快、力氣大，有尖爪利牙可以獵食。

很多動物的體色或身形可與周遭環境融為一體，保護色就是一個很好的例子。雪地動物常為白毛，森林動物多為棕毛。有些動物如變色龍，甚至可以經常變色融入環境，當這些動物靜止不動時，掠食者可能無法看見牠們。

有些動物則會利用擬態避免遭到其他動物捕食。擬態就是把自己變成其他種生物或物體的樣子。石頭魚長得像石頭，灰蝶翅膀上的斑點看起來像貓頭鷹的眼睛，偽裝成蛇的毛毛蟲看起來就像真的蛇一樣。

- **Main Idea and Details**

1 **(b)**　　2 **(b)**　　3 **(c)**　　4 **(a)**

5 a. **tongue**　　b. **camouflage**　　c. **mimicry**

6 a. **tongues**　b. **color**　c. **snowy**　d. **butterfly**　e. **snake**

- **Vocabulary Builder**

1 **adaptation** 適應　　　2 **camouflage** 偽裝；保護色

3 **predator** 掠食者　　　4 **mimicry** 擬態

A

1 **fertilized**　　　　　　　2 **go through**
3 **Mammals**　　　　　　　4 **rates**
5 **metamorphosis**　　　　6 **stages**
7 **hatches**　　　　　　　　8 **butterfly**

B

1 **respond**　　　　　　　　2 **adapted**
3 **instinctive**　　　　　　4 **behaviors**
5 **organism**　　　　　　　6 **tongues**
7 **surroundings**　　　　　8 **avoid**

C

1 **life cycle** 生命週期　　　　　2 **instinct** 本能；天性
3 **metamorphosis**（動物的）變態　4 **caterpillar** 毛毛蟲
5 **mimicry** 擬態　　　　　　　　6 **camouflage** 偽裝；保護色

D

1 受精卵 **j**　　　　　　　2 經歷 **a**
3 吐絲 **h**　　　　　　　　4 本能；天性 **e**
5 行為 **d**　　　　　　　　6 習得行為 **f**
7 冬眠 **c**　　　　　　　　8 適應 **g**
9 變色龍 **i**　　　　　　　10 擬態 **b**

17 What Changes Earth's Surface? 地表改變的原因為何？

地球表面不斷在改變，有些改變非常緩慢，有些卻非常快速。

其中一種變化由風化所造成，這是大塊岩石經年累月被分解成小顆粒的過程。風化的方式有很多種。急流和強風可以風化岩石，溫度的改變和某些化學物質也可能風化岩石。通常，風化作用的發生需要經過一段很長的時間。

侵蝕作用發生在風化之後。當被風化的岩石或土壤被帶到其他地方時，就發生了侵蝕。一般來說，風、水和冰河會造成侵蝕。如同風化作用，侵蝕通常也是一個緩慢的過程。舉例來說，科羅拉多河花了數百萬年才造就大峽谷，這屬於水侵蝕。風侵蝕會帶走珍貴的土壤，使大地化為沙漠。冰河是大型的移動冰塊，它會將行經路徑上的石頭和其他物體帶走。

• **Main Idea and Details**

1 **(b)**　　2 **(a)**　　3 **(c)**　　4 **(b)**　　5 **(c)**
6 a. **breaking**　b. **chemicals**　c. **weathered**　d. **process**

• **Vocabulary Builder**

1 **erosion** 侵蝕；侵蝕作用　　2 **weathering** 風化；風化作用
3 **glacier** 冰河　　　　　　　　4 **chemical** 化學物質

18 Fast Changes to Earth's Surface 地表的快速改變

風化和侵蝕通常需要數千年的時間才能改變地貌。然而，地震、火山和其他惡劣的天氣，卻能迅速改變地貌。

地震是地殼板塊突然移動所造成的地表震動，可導致陸地產生重大變化，例如造成陸地下降或上升，地震能使高山崩塌，甚至改變河川或溪流的路徑。

火山也可能立即改變地貌。當火山爆發時，熔岩和其他物質流至地表，這些物質會堆積成山，許多海底火山甚至能在地球的海洋中央形成島嶼。

颶風、龍捲風和洪水也會快速改變地貌。颶風會帶來強風豪雨。龍捲風則是強烈的暴風，會摧毀路徑上的大部分物體。洪水會沖刷岩石和土壤。這些猛烈的天氣型態只需要幾秒或幾小時便能改變陸地。

• **Main Idea and Details**

1 **(c)**　　2 **(c)**　　3 **(b)**　　4 **(b)**
5 a. **An earthquake is the shaking of Earth's surface caused by the sudden movement of rock in the crust.**
　b. **Underwater volcanoes can create islands in the middle of Earth's oceans.**
　c. **Floods can carry away rocks and soil.**
6 a. **rise**　　b. **lava**　　c. **Hurricanes**　　d. **Floods**

• **Vocabulary Builder**

1 **collapse** 使倒塌；使崩潰　　2 **lava** 熔岩
3 **route** 路線；路徑　　　　　　4 **erupt** 噴出；爆發

19 Our Solar System 我們的太陽系

太陽系由太陽和環繞太陽運行的一切物體所構成，包括行星、衛星和小行星。太陽是我們太陽系裡最大的物體。

行星可被分為兩組：內行星和外行星。內行星是最靠近太陽的四個行星：水星、金星、地球和火星。外行星是木星、土星、天王星和海王星，它們距離太陽較遠。

內行星全都具有堅硬地表，體積比外行星小，衛星數量都不超過兩顆。

外行星全都體積龐大，大部分由氣體組成，常被稱為氣態巨行星。所有的外行星都有許多衛星。它們周圍也環繞著由塵埃、冰塊或石頭所構成的星環。

小行星帶將內行星和外行星分隔，位於木星和火星之間。

• **Main Idea and Details**

1 **(c)**　　2 **(a)**　　3 **(c)**　　4 **(b)**
5 a. **They are Mercury, Venus, Earth, and Mars.**
　b. **They have rocky surfaces, are small, and have no more than two moons.**
　c. **They are Jupiter, Saturn, Uranus, and Neptune.**
6 a. **Earth**　　b. **moons**　　c. **gas giants**　　d. **rings**

• **Vocabulary Builder**

1 **planet** 行星　　　　　　2 **orbit** 環繞（天體等的）軌道運行
3 **outer planets** 外行星　　4 **asteroid belt** 小行星帶

20 The Sun and Other Stars 太陽和其他星體

我們的太陽系除了繞行太陽的行星以外，還有許多其他天體，其中兩種為小行星和彗星。

小行星是環繞太陽運行、由岩石組成的小天體，許多分布在火星和木星之間的小行星帶。

彗星是混合冰、岩石和塵埃的球體，它們也環繞著太陽運行。有時候，當它們接近太陽時，部分冰塊會揮發為氣體，使彗星產生長達數百萬公里的彗尾。

你還能在天空中看見哪些天體呢？我們可以在夜空中看到無數的星星，它們的大小、年齡和顏色各異。有些星群好似在夜空中構成一些形狀，我們稱之為星座。北斗七星和小北斗星是兩個著名的星座。宇宙中還有許多星系，內含著數十億顆星體。我們的太陽系正位於銀河系的邊緣。

- **Main Idea and Details**

1 **(c)**   2 **(a)**   3 **(c)**   4 **(a)**   5 **(b)**

6 a. **rocky**   b. **dirt**   c. **tails**   d. **form**

- **Vocabulary Builder**

1 **celestial object** 天體   2 **tail** 尾巴

3 **edge** 邊緣   4 **galaxy** 星系

Vocabulary Review 5

A

1 **broken**   2 **weather**

3 **weathered**   4 **erosion**

5 **collapse**   6 **instantly**

7 **surface**   8 **windstorms**

B

1 **solar system**   2 **Mercury**

3 **gases**   4 **separates**

5 **Asteroids**   6 **mixtures**

7 **well-known**   8 **Galaxy**

C

1 **erosion** 侵蝕；侵蝕作用   2 **earthquake** 地震

3 **lava** 熔岩   4 **moon** 衛星

5 **constellation** 星座   6 **comet** 彗星

D

1 風化；風化作用 **j**   2 使風化 **i**

3 帶走；搬走 **f**   4 激烈的；猛烈的 **g**

5 路線；路徑 **b**   6 衛星 **c**

7 岩石構成的；多岩石的 **e**   8 小行星帶 **h**

9 天體 **a**   10 星系 **d**

21 What Is Matter? 何謂物質？

宇宙萬物皆由物質所構成。什麼是物質呢？物質是任何佔有空間、具有質量的物體。所有氣體、液體和固體都由物質組成。

我們可以透過物質的性質來描述它們。觀察它們的顏色、大小、形狀、體積和質量，就可以分辨出各種物質。

所有物質都由各種元素組成。元素是構成宇宙間所有物質的基本成分，一共有超過一百種不同的元素，常見的有氫、氧、氮和氦。

元素結合可形成化合物，化合物是由兩個以上的元素經由化學反應結合而成的物質，例如，水是由氫和氧兩種元素組成的化合物。

所有的元素都由原子組成，原子是最小的物質粒子，兩個以上的原子結合可產生分子。

- **Main Idea and Details**

1 **(a)**   2 **(b)**   3 **(c)**   4 **(c)**

5 a. **Matter is anything that takes up space and has mass.**

   b. **There are more than 100 elements.**

   c. **Water is a compound made up of hydrogen and oxygen.**

6 a. **space**   b. **volume**   c. **basic**   d. **compounds**

- **Vocabulary Builder**

1 **element** 元素   2 **property** 特性

3 **compound** 化合物   4 **atom** 原子

22 Changes in Matter 物質的變化

物質常經歷許多變化，主要有兩種：物理變化和化學變化。

物理變化是不會產生新物質的變化。物質的物理變化有很多種型態，舉例來說，水有固態、液態或氣態，雖然每個狀態看起來都不同，但仍然是同一種物質。製作溶液也屬於物理變化的例子，如果你將鹽倒入水中並加以攪拌，鹽就會溶解，肉眼已經看不到鹽，但鹽仍然在水中。

物質也可能經歷化學變化，化學變化將會產生新的化合物。舉例來說，氫和氧通常是兩種不同的氣體，但如果將兩個氫原子跟一個氧原子結合，會形成水，這就是化學變化。

- **Main Idea and Details**

1 **(b)**   2 **(a)**   3 **(b)**   4 **(c)**

5 a. **states**   b. **physical**   c. **chemical**

6 a. **states**   b. **solution**   c. **compound**   d. **water**

- **Vocabulary Builder**

1 **chemical change** 化學變化   2 **dissolve** 溶解

3 **physical change** 物理變化   4 **stir** 攪拌

23 Taking Care of Our Bodies 照顧我們的身體

我們有時會生病，可能會感冒、染上流感或其他疾病。這些疾病都是由病毒或細菌這類微生物所造成。

生病時，我們通常會去看醫生。醫生可能給我們打針或是開藥，通常幾天後就會好轉。

然而，許多疾病，像是一般性感冒或是流行性感冒，可能會互相傳染。我們需要力行良好的健康習慣，才能維持健康、強健體魄。

首先，我們要有良好的衛生習慣，應該常洗手，用完洗手間和飯前都要洗手。

另外，我們要運動。運動可以讓我們身體健壯，也能幫助我們抵抗疾病。

均衡飲食也非常重要。健康的食物能提供身體運作的能量。不健康的食物，如垃圾食物，則可能讓你時常生病。

- **Main Idea and Details**

1 **(a)**   2 **(c)**   3 **(c)**   4 **(a)**   5 **(b)**

6 a. **bathroom**   b. **fight**   c. **energy**   d. **sick**

• Vocabulary Builder

1 **the flu** 流行性感冒　　　2 **virus** 病毒

3 **shot** 注射　　　4 **junk food** 垃圾食物

24 The Six Nutrients 六大營養素

人體需要營養素才能正常運作，營養素是食物裡的成分，身體利用它們來發育和維持健康。

一共有六大營養素，分別是碳水化合物、蛋白質、脂質、維生素、礦物質和水。每種營養素各以不同的方式幫助人體。

碳水化合物是人體能量的主要來源，可分為糖類和澱粉類兩種。含有澱粉的食物包括米飯、馬鈴薯和麵包。糖類則存在於蘋果、柳橙等水果中。

蛋白質是人體所有活細胞的組成成分，人體需要大量蛋白質來發育和修復身體細胞。肉、魚、奶、蛋和乳製品都含有蛋白質。

脂質幫助身體利用其他營養素並儲存能量。但是人體只需要少量的脂質，可從肉類、奶油、牛奶和油品中攝取脂質。

維生素可以保護身體遠離疾病。礦物質則可強化血液、肌肉和神經系統。

水有助於身體代謝廢物，同時能維持正常體溫。人不喝水甚至活不過一星期。

• Main Idea and Details

1 **(c)**　　2 **(b)**　　3 **(c)**　　4 **(b)**

5 a. **starches**　　b. **proteins**　　c. **vitamins**

6 a. **energy**　　b. **cells**　　c. **store**　　d. **nervous**　　e. **normal**

• Vocabulary Builder

1 **carbohydrate** 碳水化合物　　2 **vitamin** 維生素

3 **protein** 蛋白質　　4 **dairy product** 乳製品

Vocabulary Review 6

A

1 space　　2 described

3 elements　　4 molecule

5 substance　　6 solution

7 involve　　8 combine

B

1 cold　　2 germs

3 hygiene　　4 junk food

5 function　　6 Carbohydrates

7 repair　　8 normal

C

1 **substance** 物質　　2 **molecule** 分子

3 **chemical change** 化學變化　　4 **virus** 病毒

5 **shot** 注射　　6 **fat** 脂肪；脂質

D

1 佔據 **b**　　2 特性 **g**

3 溶解 **c**　　4 包含；牽涉 **f**

5 結合 **a**　　6 疾病 **j**

7 衛生 **h**　　8 碳水化合物 **d**

9 蛋白質 **e**　　10 移動；移除 **i**

Wrap-Up Test 2

A

1 life cycle　　2 larva

3 instinctive　　4 match

5 process　　6 carried away

7 thousands　　8 inner

9 gas giants　　10 Fats

B

1 孵化　　2（動物的）變態

3 毛毛蟲　　4 繭

5 偽裝；保護色　　6 受精卵

7 吐絲　　8 本能；天性

9 行為；態度　　10 冬眠

11 適應　　12 擬態

13 侵蝕；侵蝕作用　　14 噴出；爆發

15 星座　　16 風化；風化作用

17 使風化　　18 帶走；搬走

19 激烈的；猛烈的　　20 路線；路徑

21 衛星　　22 小行星帶

23 天體　　24 星系

25 佔據　　26 特性

27 溶解　　28 包含；牽涉

29 衛生　　30 元素

25 Fractions 分數

有時我們會將整數均分，我們可以用分數來表達這些數字。舉例來說，如果把某樣東西分為二等分，我們就說其中一半是 $\frac{1}{2}$，寫成文字就是「二分之一」，如果把某樣東西分為三等分，每一等分就是 $\frac{1}{3}$，寫成文字是「三分之一」。

分數有上下兩個數字，上面的數字是分子，下面的數字是分母。分母代表全部有多少等分，分子代表我們要數幾等分。

帶分數由一個整數和一個分數組成，$1\frac{1}{2}$、$2\frac{3}{4}$、和 $3\frac{4}{5}$ 都是帶分數。

還有所謂的等值分數，是數值相同，但用不同數字表示的分數。$\frac{1}{2}$ 和 $\frac{2}{4}$ 是等值分數，$\frac{2}{3}$ 和 $\frac{6}{9}$ 也是等值分數。

分子是 1 的分數，如 $\frac{1}{2}$ 和 $\frac{1}{3}$，叫做單位分數。

• Main Idea and Details

1 **(b)**　　2 **(a)**　　3 **(b)**　　4 **(c)**

5 a. **three**　　b. **mixed**　　c. **equivalent**

6 a. **equal**　　b. **bottom**　　c. **combinations**
　　d. **values**　　e. **numerator**

• Vocabulary Builder

1 **numerator** 分子　　2 **denominator** 分母

3 **mixed number** 帶分數　　4 **equivalent fractions** 等值分數

26 Understanding Fractions
瞭解分數之應用

❶ 這裡有一個圓，寫出它被均分為幾份，以及深色部分的分數形式。

解答：有六等分，深色部分是全部的 $\frac{3}{6}$（六分之三）。

❷ 比較 $\frac{1}{4}$ 和 $\frac{2}{4}$，哪一個比較大？

解答：$\frac{2}{4}$ 大於 $\frac{1}{4}$。當兩個分數的分母相同時，分子大的數值較大。

❸ 比較 $\frac{1}{4}$ 和 $\frac{1}{8}$，哪一個比較大？

解答：$\frac{1}{4}$ 大於 $\frac{1}{8}$。如果要比較或加總兩個分母不同的分數時，必須先把它們化為同分母。$\frac{1}{4}$ 和 $\frac{2}{8}$ 是等值分數，$\frac{1}{4}$ 等於 $\frac{2}{8}$，故 $\frac{2}{8}$ 大於 $\frac{1}{8}$。

❹ 媽媽把一顆蘋果切成很多塊，她給辛蒂 $\frac{1}{4}$ 顆，給珍 $\frac{1}{2}$ 顆。試問，誰拿到的蘋果比較大塊？

解答：$\frac{1}{2}$ 大於 $\frac{1}{4}$（$\frac{1}{2}$ 等於 $\frac{2}{4}$，故 $\frac{2}{4}$ 大於 $\frac{1}{4}$）。
由此可知，珍拿到的蘋果比較大塊。

❺ 大衛訂了一個披薩，並且切成 12 片，他自己拿了 $\frac{1}{3}$ 的披薩，史提夫拿了 $\frac{1}{4}$。試問，他們總共拿了多少披薩？

解答：$\frac{1}{3}$ 等於 $\frac{4}{12}$，$\frac{1}{4}$ 等於 $\frac{3}{12}$。由此可知，$\frac{4}{12} + \frac{3}{12} = \frac{7}{12}$。
他們總共拿了 $\frac{7}{12}$ 的披薩。

• **Main Idea and Details**

1 (a)　　　2 (a)　　　3 (c)　　　4 (c)　　　5 (b)

6 a. The one with the greater numerator is the greater fraction.
b. They are equivalent fractions.
c. There are eight equal parts.

• **Vocabulary Builder**

1 **shaded** 色彩較暗的　　　2 **compare** 比較
3 **solution** 解答　　　4 **slice** 切；把……切成薄片

27 Understanding Decimals
瞭解小數的意義

你可以把分數 $\frac{1}{10}$ 寫成小數 0.1，在 1 左邊的點叫做小數點。

小數是小數點右邊一個或一個以上的數字。小數點右邊第一位是十分位，第二位是百分位，分數 $\frac{1}{100}$ 可寫成小數 0.01。小數點右邊第三位是千分位，分數 $\frac{1}{1000}$ 可寫成小數 0.001。你可以說 $\frac{1}{1000}$ 等於 0.001。

位數	個位		十分位	百分位	千分位
	0	.	1		
值	0	.	0	1	
	0	.	0	0	1

你可以將帶分數 $1\frac{2}{10}$ 寫成小數 1.2。帶分數 $2\frac{15}{100}$ 是小數 2.15。

位數	個位		十分位	百分位
	1	.	2	
值	2	.	1	5

如同以上所述，你可以把小數轉變為等值的分數，也能將分數轉變為等值的小數。讓我們來練習把小數轉為等值分數，並把分數轉為等值小數。

1. 0.4 = ($\frac{4}{10}$)　　2. $\frac{4}{100}$ = (0.04)
3. 0.78 = ($\frac{78}{100}$)　　4. $1\frac{30}{100}$ = (1.30)

• **Main Idea and Details**

1 (a)　　　2 (b)　　　3 (c)　　　4 (a)

5 a. It is called the decimal point.
b. You can write $\frac{1}{1000}$.
c. It is the hundredths place.

6 a. Tenths place　b. third place　c. fractions　d. $\frac{1}{100}$

• **Vocabulary Builder**

1 **decimal point** 小數點　　　2 **digit** 數字
3 **tenths place** 十分位　　　4 **ones place** 個位

28 Reading and Writing Fractions and Decimals
分數和小數的讀法與寫法

分數或小數的讀寫有時看似複雜難懂，但其實非常簡單。

以分數來說，最簡單的唸法是將分子唸成基數，分母唸成序數。因此，$\frac{1}{4}$ = 四分之一，$\frac{4}{9}$ = 九分之四，$\frac{7}{15}$ = 十五分之七。

但是分數還有其他說法，你可以把 $\frac{3}{4}$ 唸成四分之三，或說四取三、三除以四。同理，$\frac{2}{3}$ 可以唸成三分之二，或說三取二、二除以三。

小數的唸法就更簡單了，只要分別唸出每個數字就行。舉例來說，2.1 就是二點一，3.14 就是三點一四。如果小數點前面有零，必須將它唸出來，例如 0.1 就是零點一。

有些小數也可以讀成分數，例如，0.5 是零點五或二分之一，0.33 就是零點三三或三分之一。

• **Main Idea and Details**

1 (a)　　　2 (c)　　　3 (c)　　　4 (b)

5 a. $\frac{2}{3}$　　b. four　　c. point

6 a. numerator　b. ninths　c. divided　d. zero

• **Vocabulary Builder**

1 **zero** 零　　　2 **cardinal number** 基數
3 **ordinal number** 序數　　　4 **individually** 單獨地；個別地

Vocabulary Review 7

A

1 equal parts　　　2 divided
3 combination　　　4 equal
5 whole　　　6 greater
7 Compare　　　8 slices

B

1 decimal　　　2 digits
3 hundredths　　　4 equivalent
5 cardinal　　　6 individually
7 decimal point　　　8 fractions

C

1 **numerator** 分子　　　　　　2 **mixed number** 帶分數

3 **tenth place** 十分位　　　　4 **ordinal number** 序數

5 **cardinal number** 基數　　　6 **digit** 數字

D

1 分子 **c**　　　　　　　　　2 單位分數 **e**

3 色彩較暗的 **g**　　　　　　4 比較 **f**

5 等值的 **j**　　　　　　　　6 切；把……切成薄片 **d**

7 十分位 **h**　　　　　　　　8 與……相等的 **b**

9 令人困惑的 **i**　　　　　　10 單獨地；個別地 **a**

29　Norse Mythology 北歐神話

北歐神話描述位於西北歐的斯堪地那維亞諸國的故事。現在的斯堪地那維亞包括挪威、瑞典、芬蘭和丹麥。

很久以前，許多維京人住在斯堪地那維亞半島，又稱為古斯堪地那維亞人。如同古希臘人和羅馬人一樣，維京人擁有自己的神話和傳說。今日，我們稱這些故事為北歐神話。

北歐神話裡有許多男女神祇，主神是奧丁，祂身上一直跟著兩隻渡鴉，分別代表「思維」和「記憶」。雷神索爾是奧丁之子，祂只要揮舞手中的巨鎚，就能使大地雷電交加、傾盆大雨。洛基是欺騙大師。奧丁的妻子弗麗嘉和索爾的妻子弗蕾亞是兩位重要女神。此外尚有其他許多男女諸神。

北歐眾神所居住的世界叫做阿斯嘉特，祂們和霜巨人、侏儒等怪物征戰不休。維京人相信名為尤克特拉希爾的「世界之樹」是支撐世界的巨樹。遲早有一天，這棵巨樹會倒下，而世界也將隨之傾倒，並引發眾神和巨人間的大戰。最後，巨人會在諸神的黃昏中贏得戰爭，世界也終將毀滅，這就是北歐神話裡的世界末日。

- **Main Idea and Details**

1 **(a)**　　　2 **(b)**　　　3 **(b)**　　　4 **(c)**　　　5 **(b)**

6 a. **chief**　　b. **thunder**　　c. **Asgard**　　d. **world tree**

- **Vocabulary Builder**

1 **Viking** 維京人　　　　　2 **Norse** 古斯堪地那維亞的

3 **thunderbolt** 雷電　　　　4 **trickster** 騙子；策略家

30　Loki the Trickster 欺騙大師洛基

洛基是北歐神話裡的欺騙大師，也是巨狼芬里爾和死神赫爾的父親。洛基時常給眾神招惹許多麻煩，尤其是索爾。但他也會獻計幫助祂們。

有一天，霜巨人索列姆偷了索爾的雷神之鎚，並說只要將索爾之妻弗蕾亞嫁給他，就願意歸還神鎚。弗蕾亞不肯答應，因此洛基出了一個主意，要索爾答應索列姆的提議，但弗蕾亞不必真的嫁給索列姆，而是聯手捉弄一下霜巨人。

洛基假扮成弗蕾亞的僕人，而索爾假扮成弗蕾亞，一同前往巨人的國度。到那裡，洛基告訴巨人們，弗蕾亞已經準備好嫁給索列姆，但新娘其實是索爾偽裝的。在婚宴上，索爾大吃又大喝，洛基趕緊解釋道：「弗蕾亞對於結婚太興奮了，所以非常飢餓。」索列姆想要親吻弗蕾亞，當他掀起新娘的面紗，卻看

見了索爾的紅眼，洛基又趕緊解釋道：「弗蕾亞因為太興奮，已經連續八天沒睡覺，眼睛才會充滿血絲。」

在婚禮上，索列姆拿出神鎚給假的「弗蕾亞」時，索爾迅速搶過神鎚，並殺死了所有的巨人。

- **Main Idea and Details**

1 **(a)**　　　2 **(c)**　　　3 **(b)**　　　4 **(a)**

5 a. **Loki was the father of both Fenrir and Hel.**

　b. **He wanted to marry Freya.**

　c. **He killed all of the giants.**

6 a. **hammer**　　b. **marry**　　c. **trick**　　d. **dressed up**

- **Vocabulary Builder**

1 **refuse** 拒絕　　　　　　　2 **servant** 僕人

3 **dress up** 裝扮　　　　　　4 **frost** 霜

31　What Kind of Sentence Is It?　英文句子種類

當我們說話時，會使用四種不同的句子，分別是直述句、疑問句、祈使句和感嘆句。

直述句用來陳述一件事，因此也被稱為陳述句。我們會在直述句的結尾加上句號，例如：

▶ 我喜歡英文。

▶ 強森先生住在都市裡。

▶ 鉛筆盒裡有三支鉛筆。

疑問句用來提問，又稱為問句，通常問號結尾，例如：

▶ 現在幾點？

▶ 你要去哪裡？

▶ 我長大以後會做什麼呢？

祈使句或命令句用來表達命令或指示。祈使句的主詞是「你」，但會被省略。這些句子以句號或驚嘆號結尾，例如：

▶ 開門。

▶ 安靜！

▶ 馬上回家。

感嘆句用來表達驚訝或興奮之情，以驚嘆號結尾，例如：

▶ 太驚人了！

▶ 我真不敢相信！

▶ 唉唷！

- **Main Idea and Details**

1 **(a)**　　　2 **(c)**　　　3 **(b)**　　　4 **(b)**

5 a. **declarative**　　b. **Interrogative**　　c. **surprise**

6 a. **period**　　b. **question mark**　　c. **orders**　　d. **exclamations**

- **Vocabulary Builder**

1 **interrogative sentence / question** 疑問句

2 **declarative sentence / statement** 直述句

3 **exclamatory sentence / exclamation** 感嘆句

4 **imperative sentence / command** 祈使句

32 Punctuation Marks 標點符號

英文裡有許多不同的標點符號，分別在不同場合裡使用。

一個句子的句末一定要加標點符號。大多數句子以句號結束
（.）。然而如果是問句，就要使用問號（?）結尾。如果是感嘆
句，就要使用驚嘆號（!）來結束句子。

但是我們也會在句子的中間使用標點符號。逗號（,）是常見的
一個標點符號，用來表示句子中間的停頓。下列句子都需要逗
號：

▶ 我喜歡吃蘋果、柳橙和香蕉。
▶ 艾瑞克是學生，而約翰是老師。

冒號（:）用來列舉事物或補充說明，例如：

▶ 冒號的用法有很多種：可用來條列或補充說明。

破折號（—）用來表示句中的停頓，例如：

▶ 杰——我的兄弟——馬上就要去做他的家庭作業了。

引號（" "）用來引述一個人的話，例如：

▶ 他說：「請開門。」

還有許多其他的標點符號，像是分號（;）、連字號（-）和
斜線（/）。

• **Main Idea and Details**

1 **(c)**　　2 **(a)**　　3 **(b)**　　4 **(a)**　　5 **(a)**
6 a. **Period**　　b. **pause**　　c. **Dash**　　d. **Semicolon**

• **Vocabulary Builder**

1 **punctuation mark** 標點符號　　2 **colon** 冒號
3 **quotes** 引號　　　　　　　　　4 **hyphen** 連字號

Vocabulary Review 8

A

1 Scandinavian　　　　　2 chief
3 Asgard　　　　　　　　4 held up
5 trickster　　　　　　　6 hammer
7 dressed up　　　　　　8 grabbed

B

1 declarative　　　　　　2 questions
3 directions　　　　　　　4 surprised
5 marks　　　　　　　　　6 period
7 pause　　　　　　　　　8 colon

C

1 **Viking** 維京人　　　　2 **thunderbolt** 雷電
3 **trickster** 騙子
4 **imperative sentence / command** 祈使句；命令句
5 **quotes** 引號　　　　6 **battle** 戰鬥；戰役

D

1 傳說；傳奇故事 **f**　　2 拒絕 **b**
3 裝扮 **c**　　　　　　　4 捉弄……；對……惡作劇 **a**
5 直述句 **d**　　　　　　6 感嘆句 **j**
7 祈使句；命令句 **i**　　8 標點符號 **h**
9 逗號 **g**　　　　　　　10 問號 **e**

33 Appreciating Artwork 藝術欣賞

博物館和畫廊展出各種不同的畫作。在許多博物館和畫廊裡，
你可以欣賞到偉大的藝術品，稱為名作。

要成為名作需要哪些條件呢？一幅畫裡有許多元素，很多畫作
運用了光影和亮色暗色對比。線條、形狀和空間感也很重要。
寫實主義和抽象主義藝術家運用線條、形狀和空間等元素的方
法就不同。

許多繪畫又有分前景、背景和中景。前景是最靠近你的物體。
在一幅畫裡，前景的物體比較大，顏色也比其他物體明亮。背
景是距離你最遠的物體，它們看起來較小。中景是介於前景和
背景之間的物體。這種透視畫法讓畫作看起來更寫實。

每幅畫裡都包含這些不同的元素，藝術大師將這些元素以最平
衡的方式運用在畫作裡，創造出偉大的作品。

• **Main Idea and Details**

1 **(b)**　　2 **(a)**　　3 **(c)**　　4 **(a)**
5 a. **Many paintings have contrasts between light and
shadows and bright colors and dark colors.**
　 b. **The foreground is the objects that are closest
to you.**
　 c. **The middle ground is those objects that are
between the foreground and the background.**
6 a. **shadows**　b. **realistic**　c. **Background**　d. **masterpieces**

• **Vocabulary Builder**

1 **masterpiece** 名作；名著　　2 **art gallery** 美術館；畫廊
3 **foreground** 前景　　　　　4 **perspective** 透視畫法

34 Creating Designs 藝術設計

藝術家在創作時，會運用線條、形狀和顏色來設計他們的作
品。「對稱」和「平衡」就是運用了線條和形狀的兩大特徵。

古希臘人創作出許多美麗的繪畫、建築和雕刻，他們的藝術成
就深深影響了後來的藝術家。古希臘人認為平衡和比例是最重
要的藝術特質，因此古希臘建築物非常講求平衡和對稱。對稱
和平衡使一件物品化為更優秀的藝術佳作。帕德嫩神廟就是最
著名的對稱建築。

顏色是另一項設計要素。色彩有三原色：紅、黃和藍。將原色
兩兩混合，會得到橙、綠和紫三種二次色。互補色是色環裡相
對的顏色，紅和綠是搭配的互補色，藍和橘還有黃和紫也是互
補色。

• **Main Idea and Details**

1 **(b)**　　2 **(a)**　　3 **(c)**　　4 **(b)**
5 a. **Greeks**　　b. **Parthenon**　　c. **secondary**
6 a. **balanced**　b. **Parthenon**
　 c. **Primary**　　d. **Complementary**

• **Vocabulary Builder**

1 **symmetry** 對稱　　　　2 **primary color** 原色
3 **proportion** 比例　　　　4 **complementary colors** 互補色

35 Elements of Music 音樂的元素

作曲家在寫曲的時候會使用特別的符號，叫做音符。音符讓我們知道樂音的節拍和長度。此外，作曲家將音符或高或低的擺在五線譜上，好讓我們知道音高——音符的高低。

當你把這些音符連續唱出或演奏時，你就在演唱或演奏一個音階。一個音階有七個主要的音符：A、B、C、D、E、F 和 G。音階上的音符各有不同的音高。音階又有大調和小調之分。

還有所謂的升記號和降記號，升記號表示一個音符的音高要升半音，降記號表示一個音符的音高要降半音。

五線譜的開端有一個特殊的記號叫做高音譜號，又名為 G 譜號。高音譜號指出 G 音符在五線譜上的位置。

• **Main Idea and Details**

1 **(c)**　　2 **(a)**　　3 **(a)**　　4 **(b)**　　5 **(a)**

6 a. **major**　　b. **Sharp**　　c. **decreases**　　d. **G clef**

• **Vocabulary Builder**

1 **composer** 作者者；作曲家　　2 **staff** 五線譜

3 **sharp note** 升記號　　4 **treble clef** 高音譜

36 Musical Instructions 音樂指導

作曲家把音符寫在五線譜上來創造樂曲，而有時他們會提供更多演奏時的具體指示。

其中兩種最普遍的指示就是連奏和斷奏。當音樂家連奏時，要流暢不間斷地演奏。而斷奏則相反，當音樂家斷奏時，要短促地一個一個音符演奏出來。

同時，音樂的力度也很重要，這是指音樂的強弱，符號標示通常是字母：p、pp、mp、f、ff 和 mf。

p 代表「弱」，意即演奏者應該柔和地演奏。pp 代表「極弱」，意即「非常柔和地」。mp 代表「中弱」，也就是「適度柔和地」。

有時候演奏者要將樂曲大聲地演奏出來。f 代表「強」，意味著演奏家應該要大聲地演奏。ff 代表「極強」，也就是「非常大聲地」。mf 代表「中強」，也就是「適度大聲地」。

另一個指示是 Da Capo al Fine。Da Capo 代表「返始」，al Fine 代表「至結尾」，Da Capo al Fine 指示演奏者要從頭重奏至 Fine 這個字為止。

• **Main Idea and Details**

1 **(b)**　　2 **(c)**　　3 **(b)**　　4 **(a)**

5 a. **Legato**　　b. **Staccato**　　c. **mezzo forte**

6 a. **Staccato**　　b. **Piano**　　c. **Forte**　　d. **repeat**

• **Vocabulary Builder**

1 **mezzo forte** 中強　　2 **staccato** 斷奏

3 **legato** 連奏　　4 **pianissimo** 極弱

A

1 exhibit	2 contrasts
3 foreground	4 balance
5 features	6 proportion
7 essential	8 color wheel

B

1 composers	2 scale
3 pitch	4 staff
5 represent	6 breaks
7 softly	8 up to

C

1 proportion 比例	2 exhibit 陳列；展覽
3 complementary colors 互補色	4 Da Capo 返始
5 musical scale 音階	6 treble clef 高音譜號

D

1 對比；對照 f	2 透視畫法 h
3 影響 a	4 認為 e
5 基本的；必要的 d	6 連續不斷地 c
7 指示；說明 g	8 斷奏 j
9 連奏 i	10 適度地；中等地 b

A

1 equal parts	2 fractions
3 greater	4 digits
5 thousandths	6 equivalent
7 Yggdrasil	8 Ragnarök
9 imperative	10 exclamatory

B

1 分母	2 分子
3 帶分數	4 小數點
5 序數	6 基數
7 數字	8 單位分數
9 與……相等	10 令人困惑的
11 分別地；逐個地	12 十分位
13 雷電	14 結婚
15 疑問句	16 引號
17 戰鬥；戰役	18 傳說；傳奇故事
19 拒絕	20 裝扮
21 捉弄……；對……惡作劇	22 直述句
23 標點符號	24 陳列；展覽
25 互補色	26 連續不斷地
27 透視畫法	28 音階
29 適度地；中等地	30 G 譜號

FÜN學 美國英語閱讀課本 5
各學科實用課文

Authors

Michael A. Putlack
Michael A. Putlack graduated from Tufts University in Medford, Massachusetts, USA, where he got his B.A. in History and English and his M.A. in History. He has written a number of books for children, teenagers, and adults.

e-Creative Contents
A creative group that develops English contents and products for ESL and EFL students.

作者	Michael A. Putlack & e-Creative Contents
翻譯	丁宥暄
編輯	丁宥榆／丁宥暄
校對	陳慧莉
製程管理	洪巧玲
發行人	黃朝萍
出版者	寂天文化事業股份有限公司
電話	+886-(0)2-2365-9739
傳真	+886-(0)2-2365-9835
網址	www.icosmos.com.tw
讀者服務	onlineservice@icosmos.com.tw
出版日期	2024 年 01 月 二版再刷（寂天雲隨身雲聽 APP 版）(080202)

國家圖書館出版品預行編目 (CIP) 資料

FUN 學美國英語閱讀課本：各學科實用課文（寂天
雲隨身聽 APP 版）/ Michael A. Putlack, e-Creative
Contents 著；丁宥暄, 鄭玉瑋譯. -- 二版 . -- [臺北市]
: 寂天文化, 2021.10-
冊；　公分

ISBN 978-626-300-050-6（第 5 冊：平裝）

1. 英語 2. 讀本

805.18　　　　　　　　　　　110012751